I0819001

JIN YOUNG IN BETWEEN

ALSO BY ELLEN OH

The Colliding Worlds of Mina Lee

ELLEN OH

CROWN
New York

Crown Books for Young Readers
An imprint of Random House Children's Books
A division of Penguin Random House LLC
1745 Broadway, New York, NY 10019
penguinrandomhouse.com
rhcbooks.com

Library of Congress Cataloging-in-Publication Data is available upon request.
ISBN 978-0-593-12598-4 (trade) — ISBN 978-0-593-12599-1 (lib. bdg.) —
ISBN 978-0-593-12599-1 (ebook)

The text of this book is set in 11.5-point Sabon Next.
Interior design by Michelle Gengaro-Kokmen

Manufactured in the United States of America
1st Printing

The authorized representative in the EU for product safety and compliance is Penguin Random House Ireland, Morrison Chambers, 32 Nassau Street, Dublin D02 YH68, Ireland, https://eu-contact.penguin.ie.

Random House Children's Books supports
the First Amendment and celebrates the right to read.

To all my fellow Kdrama romance fans
and hopeless romantics, 사랑해!

CHAPTER 1

Saying Goodbye

Jin blinked his eyes. Now he was in his room, lying in his bed. He sat up completely discombobulated. He was in a T-shirt and his boxers when just a moment ago he'd been fully dressed and in his school's gym. It had been absolute chaos: a fire on one end, debris flung everywhere, and in the middle of the room, someone had been dying. Ms. Allen, the physics teacher.

Flinging off his covers, Jin dashed over to his closet and pulled on his clothes. He needed to get back to Mina, the one person he loved more than anyone else in the world.

In the midst of pulling his jeans on, Jin froze. Mina was gone.

"I have to go now, Jin," she said. "I have to make sure that Ms. A's two little girls still have their mom."

"What are you going to do?" Jin asked in alarm.

"I have to fix it all," Mina replied. "I have to delete it."

"But what about us?"

Mina swallowed the huge lump of tears in her throat. "You'll forget about me, Jin. Everything will return to the way things were."

"You think I can forget you that easy?" Jin collapsed onto his bed. "I won't. I can't. Mina, whatever you do, I promise, I'll remember you. Always."

He closed his eyes and remembered the uncomfortable lurching sensation that had hit him deep in the pit of his stomach right before he was back in his room. It was as if everything he'd been through had been nothing more than a dream. But it wasn't. It had all been real.

It had to be. Because only since meeting Mina had Jin felt this right with the world. As if the something that had been missing his entire life had finally returned. That was who Mina was to him. The person that made him feel the most like himself. He'd never felt that way before. He wasn't sure how to go on without her.

Jin grabbed his phone. His lock screen photo that he'd taken with Mina was gone. He looked in his photo library. All the photos of Mina had disappeared. As if she'd been wiped out of his life. He was crushed. Not even one picture to remember her by. Just like his mother.

Jin winced at the thought. His mother, who thought he was dead. When Mina had first told him about his birth mother, he hadn't been able to thoroughly process all the revelations. Too much had happened too quickly. And to be honest, he couldn't think of his birth mother and what had really happened just yet. The memories were too painful to really analyze.

He looked at his phone. It read Saturday, September 10, 8:20. He'd gone back in time. Back to the time before he'd found out he'd had superpowers. Before Mina ever came to his world.

A text message alert displayed on his screen. It was from his best friend, Mark, asking Jin if he needed a ride to their ten a.m. soccer game.

Jin: hey did you hear about anything weird happening at school

Mark: weird like what?

Jin: idk students or teachers getting hurt

Mark: bruh it's Saturday
nobodys at school
why? you hear something?

Jin: no just wondering

Mark: that's weird
you need a ride to the game?

Jin paused for a long moment. The thought of seeing anyone in his current state of helpless confusion was anathema.

Jin: not gonna make it
don't feel good
tell coach for me

Mark: that sucks

Dropping his phone, Jin sat on the edge of his bed. Mark had no idea about what had happened today. He'd forgotten all about the superhero powers they'd both had and about fighting cartoonishly evil bad guys. It was proof that Mina had succeeded in completely erasing herself from his world. It meant the crazy storyline was gone and Ms. A had to be alive and well. Mina would be relieved. If only he had a way to tell her.

A numbness crept over Jin and he crawled back under his covers. His body was exhausted, but his mind was racing with thoughts. Mina had said he'd forget her once his world reset. And yet he could remember everything that had happened. Every moment he'd spent with her. Everything she had told him. Would Mina forget him also? It wasn't fair that he was the only one with any memory of what they'd all gone through.

Jin, the reason you don't see your birth mom anymore is because where I'm from, you died of cancer when you were six years old. Multiple lightning strikes hit close to your hospital room just as you died. I'm not a quantum physicist, but that anomaly might have caused the timeline to break off. It's why you woke up in the hospital alone and everyone was gone.

His brain throbbed with thoughts and visions of Mina, and his heart felt as if he'd been stabbed with a million shards of glass. Even with his eyes shut tight, he could still see her in the screen in his mind. Her long dark hair with silver-gray tips, framing her heart-shaped face. Brown expressive eyes that always seemed a little sad, that shared her every emotion, and a smile that filled up the emptiness locked deep inside him. An emptiness that now threatened to overtake him.

You're my oldest friend. We share memories and experiences that no one can take away from us, even if we're worlds apart.

Someone knocked on the door. Jin didn't move or answer, just whipped the covers over his head. The door opened and he could hear the quiet footsteps of someone walking over.

"Jin, shouldn't you wake up? Don't you have a soccer match today?" his mother asked in a low voice.

"I'm not feeling too hot," Jin muttered. "I'm gonna stay in bed."

"Oh no, do you have a fever?"

She tried to pull down his covers, but he gripped them tightly and turned away.

"Leave me alone. I just need to sleep," he snapped.

Jin listened to the quiet click of his door closing and the sound of footsteps echoing down the stairs. He was relieved his mom hadn't stayed. Correction, his adoptive mother. Strange how easy it was for Jin to suddenly start thinking of her differently. Knowing that his mother had not abandoned him had fundamentally changed him from being a sickly unwanted child to one who was truly and thoroughly loved but who had lost his family through no fault of his own or theirs.

And now his mind was filled with questions and confusion. Long-forgotten memories raced through his consciousness. His adoptive parents telling him on separate occasions how he came to be with them.

"You were always such a good boy. Never once have you given us any trouble. How could anyone have left you behind?" his adopted mother had said to him.

To make sure his adopted parents would not regret taking him in, Jin had become the perfect child. Because even at six years of age he knew that something was terribly wrong when no one came to take him home from the hospital.

That whole period was a blur to him. He didn't remember much more than the fact that he'd been very sick, sometimes delirious with pain. He remembered his birth mom's face. How she would always smile, even through her tears. How tightly she held his hand and how she showered him with kisses. But then she disappeared. Jin squeezed his eyes shut and tried to block out the memories.

He'd woken up in a hospital all alone. The doctors said he was a miracle child and wanted to study him to see how the cancer had disappeared so suddenly and completely. No one could ever explain how he'd survived. No one could have known it was because his timeline had broken off and given him a chance to live in a new world. But without his loved ones.

His entire life, he'd lived with a deep-rooted fear of being completely alone. Yet knowing that his birth mother had never meant to leave him didn't remove this fear. Instead, he found himself overcome with rage, and he didn't know why.

He was angry at his adopted parents, his birth mother, the world, at everyone. However, he was most angry at Mina for leaving him behind. Again.

Anger turned to grief.

"It would've been better if you'd never come," Jin said bleakly. "If I'd never known you and what happened in your world."

CHAPTER 2

The Professor

For months after losing Mina, Jin haunted the library, researching everything he could find about quantum physics. He wondered if what had brought Mina into his world had been some sort of wormhole. But all he could find were theories and conjecture. Nothing that could help him answer his questions.

Out of frustration, he consulted Ms. Allen, the AP Physics teacher, and posited hypothetical questions that led into discussions of parallel worlds and the probability of other universes.

"Jin, I think you should meet an old friend of mine, Albert Brennan," Ms. A said after one particularly long discussion. "He's a professor of astronomy and astrophysics at George University. I think he'd really enjoy talking to you."

Saturday, March 8

Jin went to visit the professor. Although it was chilly, the campus was full of students playing Frisbee, picnicking, or simply lounging on the expansive front lawn, taking in the bright sunshine. The buildings that formed the quadrangle were majestic and old. One even looked like a castle, with stained-glass windows. Jin walked past the historic buildings and followed a wide path to the south side of campus where the science departments were housed.

In direct contrast to the north campus, the physics department was in a modern architectural masterpiece of steel and glass that rose twelve stories high and dazzled the eye as the sun reflected off the building. Inside, there was a sweeping grand staircase surrounded by lots of tiered seating, where students both studied and slept. Jin made his way to the fifth floor and knocked on Dr. Brennan's office door.

"Come in," the professor called out.

With a warm smile, Dr. Brennan rose to shake Jin's hand before leading him to a small conference table. Bookshelves lined the wall behind a large desk stacked with folders and papers in numerous piles.

The professor was an average-sized African American man of slight build with a poufy salt-and-pepper Afro and black horn-rimmed glasses. He wore a wrinkled blue button-up shirt that was rolled at his elbows and dotted with coffee stains under his loose striped necktie. Leaning forward in his seat, Dr. Brennan gazed with wide-eyed interest at Jin.

"Tell me, why are you interested in the idea of parallel worlds?" Dr. Brennan asked.

Because I want to see Mina again. Jin pushed the thought

away. He had never been able to tell anyone about Mina and he didn't think he ever could.

"Well, it just seems egocentric to think that our world is the only one out here," Jin replied.

The professor nodded enthusiastically. "Of course! This is the whole reason we explore space. But finding life in the vastness of our universe is different from a belief in parallel worlds."

"But do you believe they're possible? And if so, how?"

Dr. Brennan smiled. "Who knows for sure? All we have are theories."

Jin had to bite his tongue to keep from yelling that he did actually know. That parallel worlds did exist. Instead he asked, "Do wormholes exist, and could they connect us to another world?"

"Theoretically, a wormhole is a tunnel between two universes that would allow for the shortest amount of time traveled between them. Basically, a shortcut. In science fiction, two black holes might form a wormhole, sort of like when Thor and Banner fly through the Devil's Anus in *Thor: Ragnarok*."

Jin cocked an eyebrow in surprise. "*Thor: Ragnarok*?"

The professor chuckled. "I'm a big Avengers fan, although technically the Devil's Anus would have been too unstable to fly a spacecraft through. It would have collapsed the minute they tried to pass through it."

Jin was trying to remember the scene in the movie that Dr. Brennan was talking about. There had been something that looked like a massive tornado with a red volcanic hole on the bottom of it.

"That's what a wormhole looks like?" he asked.

"Well, Banner called it a collapsing neutron star inside an Einstein-Rosen bridge, which is pure science fiction." Dr. Brennan grinned. "He's describing a supernova that would collapse into a black hole inside a wormhole. I thought the movie rendition of it was pretty ingenious, although clearly in the realm of the impossible."

"Are any wormholes real?" Jin asked.

"Hypothetically possible, but whether or not matter could actually pass through a wormhole is unknown. They do make for great visual effects!"

So not a wormhole, then, Jin thought. But how had Mina's world connected with his?

"Instead of a wormhole, what about quantum tunneling?" Dr. Brennan asked. "It's a phenomenon that allows a particle to penetrate a seemingly impossible barrier and appear instantly on the other side. But it is a theory that applies at the quantum level. For humans to travel to another world would seemingly be impossible, as we are much larger than a particle. It would only work if you were Ant-Man at a subatomic level."

"Ant-Man." Jin sighed. "You really like your Marvel movies, huh."

"They're a perfect vehicle for visualizing so much of what is unknown," the professor responded as he launched into a description of a scene from *Ant-Man and the Wasp*.

Feeling discouraged by everything Dr. Brennan had said, Jin ignored the professor's recap of the movie. "So there's no explanation."

The professor clasped his hands together and leaned his elbows on the table to look intently into Jin's eyes. His expression was kind but curious.

"Normally, students who talk to me about parallel worlds are excited, enthusiastic, inquisitive. But you seem troubled and morose," Dr. Brennan said. "What's bothering you?"

That I'm in a world without my mom and Mina.

An overwhelming urge to tell the professor everything rose inside Jin. He swallowed hard against it and thought carefully of what he could say that wouldn't make the professor think he was having a delusional break from reality.

"I've been having dreams that feel very real, where I'm interacting with someone from another world that's exactly like ours, except I'm not there," Jin said slowly. "But here in this world, she's the one that's missing."

"*Fascinating!* When did you start having these dreams?"

"Last September, for several weeks," Jin replied. "They were so vivid that I couldn't tell what was real and what was a dream."

"I would love to hear the details of your dream, if you don't mind," the professor said, his eyes bright with interest.

Jin hesitated, but the desire to share was too strong inside him; he let himself trust the professor. He took a deep breath and launched into a full narrative of all that had occurred to him. When he was done, Dr. Brennan seemed to be deep in thought.

"I know it sounds crazy," Jin said.

"Don't say that, Jin," Dr. Brennan responded. "Quantum physics is the science of the impossible."

The professor leaned back in his chair and tapped his nose for a moment before continuing.

"Have you ever heard of Schrödinger's cat?" Dr. Brennan asked.

Jin was unsure. "Maybe? But I don't know what it is."

"Ha!" The professor let out a loud laugh. "See, this is what happens when science fiction writers use complicated terms that they don't really explain. I think the best explanation was actually in an episode of *The Big Bang Theory*, and it had nothing to do with quantum mechanics at all—"

"So what is it?" Jin interrupted the professor before he could go off on another tangent.

"Oh, right! It's a thought experiment that is related to the many worlds theory," Dr. Brennan explained. "It starts with the idea that a quantum particle exists in multiple states at the same time until it is observed, at which point it is measured. Schrödinger posited a paradox. There's a cat in a sealed box with a timed poison that will be released under a certain set of variables. Until the box is opened and the cat is observed, we can't know what state the cat is in. Therefore, at any given moment the cat is both dead and alive."

"Huh?" Jin was confused.

"Exactly," the professor responded. "Even Schrödinger thought that was ridiculous. However, the many worlds theory says that every time you open the box, a new possibility is released. The cat is alive, but in another alternate world, the cat is dead. Now, this is all theory. Except that in your dream you are Schrödinger's cat. You are both alive and dead at the same time because you were in two different worlds."

The whole cat story was too confusing to Jin, but he was grateful that the professor did not think he was delusional.

"So there are two different worlds . . ." Jin trailed off as the professor shook his head.

"Not just two," Dr. Brennan said. "There could be an infinite number of worlds with you and Mina in them. In theory. You said that in Mina's timeline, the moment you died it caused a split that formed this world, where you live but find your friend and family gone. The multiworld theory says that since there are many different probable outcomes, there is also a world where you're still with your friend and family. There could be a world where you're in a coma. Or one where you survived but with complications or no memories, et cetera. Or you and your friend are both in the same world but you're no longer connected. And that's just branches from what happened when you were six. Other realities could have split off from different major life-changing events. There are too many variables!"

The idea of infinite worlds made Jin's head spin. This was way beyond what he could have imagined.

"Come with me. I want to show you something," Dr. Brennan said.

The professor took Jin on a tour of the large laboratory a few floors down from his office. In the noisy room, some students in white coats and goggles were taking notes as they stared up at a large wired contraption hanging from steel beams. It was a gleaming maze of silver metal tubes, gold components, and hundreds of white wires all strategically knitted together to form a bizarre but beautiful chandelier.

"This is Skybird," Dr. Brennan explained. "She's our quantum computer, and she is the answer to the question of parallel universes."

"*That's* a computer?" Jin asked in surprise.

"Yes, the reason it looks different is because of the dilution refrigerator, which is that big cylindrical device. It keeps the quantum processor, the brain of the computer, at a nice near-zero temperature."

Jin wondered why the professor was showing it to him. "But what's the purpose of Skybird?"

"That's the exciting part! We've created holographic simulations of wormholes, but Skybird is going to help us create a real traversable wormhole," Dr. Brennan said. "At least, that is our plan and why we got a ten-million-dollar grant from Tundra Labs!"

"Tundra? I've heard of them," Jin mused.

"Of course you have! They have a multibillion-dollar state-of-the-art laboratory called TULLY. It's one of the few places in the world where you can study dark matter about four thousand feet below the earth's surface, shielded from the sun and space."

"Whoa, that's so cool! Is that underground laboratory where you do your experiments?" Jin asked.

Dr. Brennan shook his head. "We aren't quite there yet. We are in the model and computation phase of the experiment. So, to answer your question about wormholes, I believe that they do exist. And I hope to prove it to the world."

Jin blinked in surprise. "But I thought you didn't believe in them."

"I didn't say that," the professor replied. "I just said the current idea of a wormhole being formed by two black holes would mean it was dangerously unstable. But a combination of quantum entanglement and tunneling might in due course create an actual wormhole."

Jin's heartbeat was suddenly loud in his ears. Maybe this was the answer he was looking for.

"We know that a single atom can quantum-tunnel through barriers," Dr. Brennan continued. "The next step is to see how entanglement might affect the size of particles that can tunnel."

"Like a person?" Jin asked hopefully.

The professor chuckled. "Eventually, maybe. But it will take time. It took fifteen years for scientists to finally see a hydrogen ion quantum tunnel."

The conversation had deflated Jin. There was no scientific answer to the question of how Mina had traveled to his world. No explanation for why his world and hers had split off.

"Jin, sometimes a thing is unexplainable," the professor said. "Not because it can't happen, but because we just don't know how it happens yet."

Feeling a bit better, Jin thanked the professor.

"Come and see me again," Dr. Brennan said as Jin left the office.

Jin took the bus home and walked to Mina's house. It was empty. No one lived there anymore. It was odd. This was a popular neighborhood for renting and owning. Especially for young families. And yet Mina's town house had remained completely empty and unlived in for months. As he stood staring, an older white woman stepped out of the next-door house.

"Excuse me," Jin asked her as she approached him. "Could you tell me when the Lee family moved out?"

The woman looked at him curiously. "The Lee family?"

"Yes, Korean American family. Father was a lawyer, mother an artist, they had a little girl named Mina. Do you know them?"

She looked very surprised. "Yes, I knew them. Lovely

family. But they moved out over ten years ago. I have no idea where they went."

"Ten years?" Jin asked.

"Yes," the woman continued. "They moved quite suddenly. Didn't even let any of the neighbors know. It was a bit shocking; that's why I remember them."

She looked back at the house. "Other than the management company that maintains it, it's almost always empty these days."

Had the house always been empty before and Jin had never realized it?

As the woman walked away, Jin gazed unhappily at Mina's town house. Mina and her family had never been in this world that had split off.

CHAPTER 3

Friends

Wednesday, March 26

"You guys are lucky!" Liam Pham, Jin's oldest friend, pushed in between Mark and Jin as they walked to lunch. "No more stressing about these stupid college acceptances!"

Jin had found out he was accepted to Johns Hopkins, while Mark had known about MIT five days earlier. It was why they were walking over to the local pizzeria for lunch. Liam had been adamant about celebrating.

At the restaurant, Liam announced, "All the pizza slices you can eat and soda refills are on me!"

"Oooooh, big spender," Mark teased as he smiled in appreciation.

They ordered double slices with soda and listened to Liam complain about his applications.

"I can't believe I still have almost a week to hear from all my schools," he griped.

"Jin's still waiting on a few, right?" Mark looked over at Jin.

"Aw, come on!" Liam cut in. "He's got the dean's scholarship to Johns Hopkins! He's all set!"

Mark shot Liam a disapproving look as he slung an arm around Jin's shoulders.

"You good?" he asked.

Jin nodded. Mark was the only one of his friends who knew how rough the last six months had been for him. For a kid who had never fought with his parents, applying to college had caused a huge rift in Jin's relationship with his adoptive family.

Of course, that wasn't entirely true. It wasn't applying to colleges that had affected their relationship; it was Mina.

Meeting Mina had changed him fundamentally. He was painfully aware that he was not where he was supposed to be. The life he had made in this world was not the one he should have had. Jin was aware of the irony of his feelings. He wouldn't even be alive if the timeline hadn't broken off and formed this new world. But that was the problem. Because Jin knew what had happened. This knowledge of what could have been colored everything: his relationships with his friends and parents, even his plans for the future.

Jin's depression over losing Mina had morphed into a sullen anger and an ugly moodiness that tested his parents' patience. They wanted to send him to therapy, just like when he'd first been adopted. It had been helpful back then, to deal with all the disruptive changes he'd gone through. But therapy couldn't solve the multiverse.

It was Mark who'd helped Jin find the words he needed to talk to his parents about all he was going through.

"What's going on?" Mark had asked. "You've been really unhappy lately. Talk to me."

Jin sighed and leaned his head back on the leather headrest of Mark's Jeep. "I just don't know what I want to do with my life anymore."

"Whoa, that's huge. You're always been serious about being pre-med. What happened?"

"I'm trying to figure out if I really want to be a doctor or if I feel like I should just because of my dad," Jin said.

"That's deep," Mark replied. "But then again, is that a bad thing? Being a doctor like your dad is?"

"The thing is, I feel like I've been acting out a part all this time. Be the good son they want me to be," Jin said. "You know, be grateful to be adopted. But why do I have to be so grateful? What did I do that was so wrong in the first place?"

Jin slammed his fist into the dashboard. "Man, I hated family outings so much because people always stare. And you can see exactly what they're thinking: wondering who I am, why I'm with this white family, where I'm really from, and how lucky I am. Then there's always that one really rude person who just has to ask if I'm adopted right in front of me."

"That's so wrong." Mark shook his head.

"The worst part is when they remind me that I'm such a lucky boy," Jin said. "I really hate people."

For the first time, Jin had put into words the detachment and unhappiness that had underscored much of his teen years. The indescribable sense of not belonging that related to being a transracial adoptee. He felt a calm relief at unburdening himself to his friend.

Mark suddenly pulled over and parked.

"I never knew you felt like this," he said. "Not that I understand what you must be going through, but it makes sense to me 'cause some people are racist. This is way deeper than I imagined. I always knew adoptees had some serious baggage, but this is some rough stuff."

"I'm sorry to dump that on you," Jin replied. "I've been feeling overwhelmed lately."

"Hey, it's not good to hold all that in, you gotta talk to someone about all this. And you know you can talk to me anytime. I'm here for you."

"Yeah, I know," Jin said. "All those years of therapy and I still missed the big issue."

"Maybe you didn't know how to talk about it before."

Jin immediately thought of Mina and the other world where she and his mother lived and how he couldn't be farther away from the two people he wanted to be with the most. He let out a sad little laugh. "I didn't even know what I was feeling until now."

"I think you need to tell your parents," Mark said.

"I don't know about that," Jin replied. "They'll just put me into therapy again, and I'm not ready to talk about this yet. I'm still processing it."

Mark pressed an awkward hand on Jin's shoulder. "Bro, I'm here for you."

After his talk with Mark, he'd explained all his emotions to his parents, and they'd been shocked, angry, and then guilt-ridden. They didn't know how to respond except to send him to therapy again, which didn't help as much when the therapist didn't really understand the unique challenges of transracial adoption. It was Mark who had helped Jin find the language he needed to come to a painful truce with his adoptive parents. Mark, who understood the challenges of navigating white spaces as a Black man, had taught Jin to be direct and honest in ways Jin had never been before. He'd learned to control his anger and resentment, and his parents had tried to understand his grief. It was awkward for everyone, leading to Jin's relief in receiving a full ride to Johns Hopkins. While his parents were willing to pay for all his schooling, Jin was grateful that he would not need to rely on them. A sentiment he'd only expressed to Mark. It was too painful to share with anyone else.

But Jin had never told anyone about Mina, not even Mark. And it was eating him up inside.

"Jin, I just don't get you lately," Liam was saying. "What is up with you? You've been in such a bad mood. You don't say much anymore. I thought it was just college apps. But you're set now, and look at you! You're still all weird and shit. I don't get it. We're your friends. Talk to us."

At Liam's words, Mark glanced at Jin and whispered, "Totally understand if you *don't* feel like talking about it now also."

"No, he needs to talk about it!"

"It might be too personal . . ."

"So?" Liam seemed perplexed. "I tell you guys everything."

"Ever thought about the fact that you shouldn't?"

"What? Why? That's what friends are for."

"Some things might need to be worked out by yourself," Mark said pointedly.

Liam narrowed his eyes. "Hey, you know something about Jin that I don't know, right?"

"Nah . . ."

"Yes, you do! You guys are keeping something from me! That's not cool!"

"Back off, Pham, it's not about you . . ."

The look of betrayal that crossed Liam's face was almost comical.

"I knew it! You are keeping something from me!"

Liam jumped to his feet and paced back and forth for a moment before sitting down again.

"I can't believe you told Mark something and not me," Liam complained as he pointed an angry finger in Jin's face.

Mark put up his hands in a placating manner. "He didn't—"

"Yes, he did! Don't lie to me." Liam glared at them both. "I can see it on both of your faces and it cuts me deep."

Liam turned sideways in his chair and took an angry swig of his soda.

"Aw, come on, Liam, don't be like that," Mark said.

Liam waved a one-fingered salute at them. "You both suck."

Jin felt a surge of affection for his two best friends. He didn't deserve them.

"Sorry, Liam," Jin said. "It's just that I finally let my family know how hard it's been for me being Asian in a white family, and as you can imagine, it caused a lot of issues."

At his words, Liam swiveled around to face Jin. "Explain in detail, and don't leave anything out."

Hesitating for a moment, Jin reluctantly shared with Liam all he'd gone through. "That's why we had to do family therapy, and things are slowly getting better. The only reason

Mark knows is because he saw me after the first huge fight I had with my folks. Otherwise, I don't know if I would have told anyone."

For once Liam was completely silent, just staring at Jin with an awkward expression.

"Don't make that face at me, you're creeping me out," Jin said with a smile.

"I had no idea what you were going through," Liam replied. "That sounds rough."

You have no idea, Jin thought. But instead, he just said, "Thanks."

A sudden urge to tell them all about Mina overcame him. What could it hurt?

"But that's not all," he continued. "I think I've been going through an existential crisis."

"Or late puberty," Liam joked.

Mark nodded. "Yeah, there's definitely something else going on. You know, Diana thinks you've been dating someone and got dumped. Have you been seeing someone that we don't know about?"

Mark and Diana were an official couple. They'd even applied to colleges in the same cities so that they could stay close during college. Something Jin had wanted to do with Mina, before he realized it was impossible.

"Yeah, I was." Jin couldn't stop himself from letting it slip out. But there was no taking it back. The weight of keeping Mina a secret had been such a heavy burden. He ached to talk to someone about her. About how much he missed her.

Liam slid onto the bench next to Jin. "What? And you didn't tell us? Who was it? Someone from school?"

"No, you guys don't know her, she goes to another school far from here."

"Did you meet her on Swipe? What's her name? Is she pretty?"

Mark put up a hand. "Hey, Pham, chill." Turning to Jin, he asked, "You wanna tell us about her?"

"Her name is Mina Lee. She was in town for a short time last fall. We dated," Jin said. "And then she went home. End of story. Except I fell real hard for her and it's been tough not seeing her anymore. I don't even have a picture of her."

"Do you guys keep in touch?"

"No."

"Why?"

"She's really far away," Jin said. "It wasn't workable."

"Man, that's harsh," Liam replied. "But how far are we talking? Chicago? Los Angeles?"

"Another world," Jin said softly.

"The other side of the world?" Liam misheard. "Like New Zealand?"

Not knowing what to say, Jin just nodded.

"Yeah, that's some serious distance," Mark responded.

"Still, it's not impossible," Liam cut in. "I mean, people have long-distance relationships all the time."

"It just wasn't going to work out," Jin said.

Liam started to say more, but Mark kicked him under the table. "Ow, what was that for?"

"Drop it," Mark warned. "Jin, if you don't want to talk about it, you don't have to."

"No, it's okay, I should have told you before, but to be honest, I just couldn't," Jin said. "It hurts to talk about her."

"I get it," Mark responded. "You don't have to say anything."

"Yeah, totally know what you're going through," Liam said.

Mark snorted. "Man, no you don't."

"Yes, I do!" Liam was indignant. "Rachel Pearson totally broke my heart last year."

"Rachel Pearson doesn't even know you exist," Mark retorted.

"And it broke me."

Jin had to laugh. He appreciated his friends' efforts to make him feel better. Maybe he should have talked to them earlier.

"Listen, I know it's hard right now, but it will get better," Mark said. "You just gotta try to forget about her."

"That's the problem, I don't want to forget about her," Jin replied.

"Then figure out how you can see her again and make it happen," Liam commented. "Even if it takes a long time. Keep trying and one day you'll see her again."

It was on the tip of Jin's tongue to tell them just why it could never happen. But Jin mentally shrugged. No one would believe him. Sometimes he even went so far as to think he had dreamed Mina up. He had no proof that she'd ever been here in the first place. That she existed at all. And it would hurt so much less if he could convince himself that it had all been a dream.

"What's her name? Mina Lee?" Liam asked. "That name sounds familiar."

Jin looked sharply at his friend. "It does?"

"I had the biggest crush on a girl named Mina Lee in kindergarten," Liam said with a nostalgic smile. "She wore her hair in these long pigtails and was always drawing pictures of animals. She was my first love."

"That's *Mina*!" Jin shouted. He couldn't believe it. Someone else remembered her.

"She was in kindergarten with us, but she must have moved away during summer break 'cause she wasn't back for first grade," Liam said.

Mina was here! Liam remembers her! Jin thought to himself in growing excitement. *Liam knew Mina!*

Mark stared at Liam in amazement. "Dude, are you serious? How do you remember a girl from kindergarten?"

"How could I forget my first love?" Liam asked. He then grinned at Jin. "Do you remember when Sam Ahmed dared me to climb to the top of the monkey bars? Once I got to the very top, I was too scared to climb down?"

"Of course I remember! You were crying so hard you started screaming and the entire playground just stared at you—"

"I was five and terrified," Liam cut in.

"You refused to climb down."

"Like I said, I was five and I was afraid I'd fall and die," Liam repeated in an aggrieved tone. "It was Mina who rescued me."

"No way!" Mark started laughing. "I wish I'd been there!"

Jin could see the scene in his head. Mina had scrambled quickly up to where Liam was and had talked to him. After a few minutes, she'd gotten him to climb down with her.

"What did she say to you?" Jin asked.

Liam smiled. "She asked me what was the matter, and I told her I was stuck. And she said, No you're not. And suddenly, I wasn't."

"That's what got you down?" Jin asked in astonishment.

"Well, it was just the way she said it. Very confidently," Liam mused. "And then she said, Come on, we'd better go before Mr. Robinson—you remember, that scary PE teacher?—comes. That got me moving real fast."

Jin remembered it all. Liam and Mina scampering down the monkey bars and then running off to play as if nothing had happened. He remembered being both awed by how Mina had helped Liam and, then, jealous that she was playing with him.

"So tell me, what does she look like now?" Liam asked. "I bet she's gorgeous, am I right?"

Jin nodded, with a smile so wide it hurt.

"She's beautiful," he said, his voice husky with emotions. "I wish I had a photo to show you."

"Well, you have to tell her hi for me if you ever talk to her again," Liam said.

Jin nodded. He felt euphoric. Mina was real. Liam knew who she was. He hadn't imagined her. And for the first time since Mina had left him, Jin felt happy.

That night, Jin dreamed of Mina again. But this time it was the most vivid dream. He was in front of Mina's house and he could hear her calling for him.

Jin, I miss you.

"Mina, I'm here!" Jin shouted as he opened the door and entered her house.

Inside, everything looked exactly as he'd seen it the other night. Except, there was no little robot to whirl around in circles beeping cheerfully at him. From upstairs, he could hear Mina crying. He followed her voice up to her room, but when he opened her door, there was nothing but darkness. He was about to turn away when he heard Mina's voice again.

"I miss you, Jin," she said.

"Mina!" Jin stepped into the room and was immediately enveloped in what felt like emptiness. It was pitch-black and completely silent. He called out Mina's name again, but his voice was swallowed up by the air around him.

What is this place? he asked himself.

He could no longer hear Mina's voice. He took another step forward and stopped. The space around him suddenly felt vast. He was afraid he'd lose himself if he went any farther.

Discouraged, he turned to leave. He could see the lit doorway he'd entered through. As he walked to it, the light flickered and he could see the fuzzy outline of someone on the other side. He heard a soft murmuring. Positive that it was Mina, he rushed forward, but just as he reached the door, the vision began to clear, and he woke up with a start, his heart pounding erratically. He felt dizzy and sick to his stomach, and yet hopeful. He wasn't sure what that was, but it didn't feel like a dream. It was so vivid and real that he couldn't help but feel like he was actually connecting to Mina. Because it meant he could possibly contact her. He just needed to come up with a plan.

CHAPTER 4

The Black Hole in the Sky

Thursday, March 27

Jin spent the morning in a bit of a daze, trying to figure out what happened last night. It felt momentous because it had occurred the same day Liam remembered Mina. Jin wanted to believe that these were signs and not just wishful thinking on his part.

At lunch, Jin went with Mark, Liam, and Sam to a nearby deli. The day was unseasonably frigid, with a brutal wind that cut through their thin jackets. Liam and Sam were arguing over their favorite basketball teams, while Mark was texting Diana. When they reached the strip mall, Jin stopped dead in his tracks. The sky looked like it had been split in half by a massive cleaver. Inside the split, Jin could see an enormous black hole that was dotted with hundreds of stars and swirling clouds.

"What the hell is that?" Jin asked.

Liam and Sam stopped to see what Jin was pointing at.

"What are we looking at?" Sam asked.

"What's that thing up there?" Jin gestured wildly at the black swirl above them.

"They're just clouds," Sam said. "You're acting kind of weird."

Jin stared bug-eyed at his friends. "You don't see a big gaping hole in the sky?"

Mark finally stopped texting.

"Are you talking about those big dark storm clouds?" Mark asked. "That's not exactly a hole, dude."

"I think he's messing with us," Sam said. "Come on, let's go. I'm starving!"

Jin was shocked and confused. Were his friends really unable to see the massive hole above them? It was far too big for them to miss it. Was he hallucinating? Grabbing his cell phone, Jin snapped several photos. But when he looked at them, the sky was completely normal. He was stunned. Right above him was a hole of swirling blackness. His cell phone, however, did not capture the scene as he saw it. Completely weirded out, Jin rushed into the deli to join his friends. When they finished eating and returned to school, he avoided looking at the sky. The anomaly was too frightening. It made him nervous and slightly scared. He wondered what was wrong with him.

As they rounded the loop in front of the building, Jin was hit with the unusual sensation of air surging around him. His stomach felt like it had jumped up into his chest, giving him intense heartburn. When it abruptly stopped, his friends were nowhere to be seen. Instead, he was surrounded by a large group of students that appeared seemingly out of the air. They carried rainbow flags and signs of protest and chanted, "This is what democracy looks like!" Jin gawked at the scene around him. He couldn't see his friends anywhere.

Pushing past the protestors, Jin tried to find Mark, Liam, and Sam. He blinked at the dark, cloud-filled sky. It was going to pour rain at any moment. But he couldn't see the strange anomaly. Perhaps it was hidden behind the clouds. Or maybe it had disappeared. His heart began pounding again. He stared at the building. It looked exactly like his school. Some of the students seemed familiar. But a thought occurred to him. This was *not* his world.

He passed students carrying signs that said NO ONE IS ILLEGAL and END FASCISM! The air was thick with anger. No matter how oblivious he was, Jin could not have missed news about a coordinated walkout by the entire student body. This was *not* his school.

Excitement bubbled up in his chest. Could he be in Mina's world? In the thick of the crowd, he couldn't see anyone. Just as he wondered where Mina might be, he felt the rapid rush of air and he was transported back to his world, under the same swirling black hole that he had been trying to escape. Only this time, the sunny skies were filled with ominous gray clouds. And yet the clouds did nothing to cover the frightening rip in the sky.

"Jin!" Liam shouted from across the street. "How the heck did you get over there?"

Jin was at a loss for words. What could he tell them? He didn't even know himself. Something incredible had just happened to him, but who would believe it?

* * *

After school, Jin had a prom committee meeting that Mark and Diana had coerced him into attending. Now he was regretting it and trying to hide from them. Craving solitude, he walked to the empty courtyard so he could process everything that had occurred to him.

Outside, his eyes were immediately drawn to the sky. He'd avoided looking out the window during afternoon classes, afraid of finding the anomaly that only he could see. But now he couldn't avoid it. There it was. A massive tear in the sky that even the dark clouds couldn't hide.

Jin shivered as a harsh, cold wind penetrated his bones—and once again he felt the sensation of his body lurching into another space. Suddenly, he was in a torrential downpour, getting drenched. Confused, he turned to go back inside and stopped short. Mina was standing in the doorway, looking up at the sky. This was not his imagination. His breath caught as he moved closer.

"Mina?"

Mina's eyes widened in surprise and her lips parted as if she was about to call his name. She extended both her arms and started forward. Not wanting her to get wet, Jin was moving toward her when the rain stopped and she vanished. Once again, he was in the chilly courtyard, but this time he was wet and shivering, his stomach still feeling queasy. Jin remained motionless as he tried to understand if he'd really seen Mina or if he'd just imagined her.

"Whoa, Jin, how'd you get all wet?" Liam stood in front of him, holding an umbrella over his head as he waved his hand in Jin's face. "Go inside before you get sick."

In a daze, Jin followed Liam inside. He was still too

stunned to speak and couldn't respond to any of Liam's questions.

"What happened to you?" Liam asked. "Jin? Hello, Jin?"

Liam shook him by the shoulders. "Dude, you'd better go home. You're really out of it."

Nodding, Jin thanked his friend and trudged down the hallway. He needed to think about what had happened. Shaking off the rain as best he could, Jin left the building. With the cold wind whipping around him, he rushed home as fast as he could.

Inside his house, he was relieved to find it empty. He would not have been up to listening to Alice worrying about his health. Jin slowly made his way to his room in the loft on the fourth floor of their town house. He stripped off his wet clothing and stared at it in utter confusion. He'd really seen Mina! This was not a figment of his imagination caused by his missing her. Somehow, he'd stepped into her world and had seen her. It was the only explanation for the change in weather that had soaked him to the bone. Somehow, he'd slipped into her world. But it had been too short. Not even the space of a minute. He needed more time to see her, talk to her, hold her.

He took a hot shower, hoping it would not only warm his body but also help clear his brain. All it did was increase the intensity of his longing to see Mina again. He was having such a hard time processing everything. His thoughts kept going round and round without making any sense. Maybe he was still in too much shock.

He was positive he'd stepped into Mina's world and seen her. Judging by the look on her face, he was sure she'd seen him too.

After his shower, he flopped onto his bed and reviewed everything that had recently occurred. So far, these weird events had happened only near or in school. That made sense. It was where Mina had first entered his life. What he didn't know was why he was being pulled into her world or how he could do it again.

From outside, Jin heard the loud crack of thunder. The next moment, the skies unleashed heavy rains that bounced hard against his windows in a cacophony of deafening beats. The sky was as dark as night and covered with clouds. Jin could no longer spot the anomaly. It had disappeared.

CHAPTER 5

Strange Worlds

Saturday, March 29

Several days later, Jin sat at a long table at the local diner with a large group of friends. It was a warm and sunny day, and everyone was in great spirits except Jin. He would rather have stayed home. Which was unusual given that he'd already been homebound because of the weather.

Two consecutive days of rain, hail, and hurricane-force winds had caused numerous electrical outages and countless traffic accidents across the city. The severe weather had shut down all schools and government agencies. When the sun had finally come out this morning, everyone had been ecstatic. Jin had been bombarded with texts and calls to grab lunch and hang out.

Which was how Jin ended up seated between Liam and Mark and across from Diana and her friends Lauren, Abby, and Tracey. All four of them had been friends with Mina when she was here. And yet none of them remembered her now.

"You all are invited to my party the weekend after graduation," Diana was saying. "It's gonna be epic! My parents are renting out one of those fancy mansions on Mass Ave."

"Must be nice, having rich parents," Liam snarked.

"I'm sorry, how many pairs of sneakers do you own? Two hundred?"

"Under a hundred. And they're a business investment. For my videos." Liam was a sneakerhead. He actually had over twenty thousand followers on his social media platform, where he would talk about his collections and how to buy and sell them.

"And where are you spending your summer again?" Diana asked with a raised eyebrow.

"That's not the same," Liam replied. "That's a forced trip to the motherland to learn about my heritage."

"At least the food will be good," Mark cut in.

"Yes!" Liam responded. "Can't wait to eat my way through Vietnam!"

The motherland. For Jin, that would be Korea. But Jin had no family to take that trip with. His parents had talked about going, but it wouldn't be the same. He wanted to go with his birth mom and Mina.

"Hey, Jin, do you have a date to prom?" Lauren asked, sending the other girls into a fit of giggles.

Feeling uncomfortable, Jin shook his head. "I'm not going."

"But you're gonna come to my graduation party, right, Jin?" Diana asked.

"Sure, wouldn't miss it," Jin replied politely.

“We should all go to prom together, as a group,” Tracey said. “We did that for homecoming and it was so much fun.”

“Yeah, Jin,” Mark said. “Help a brother out. Don’t leave me with all these girls.”

Diana smacked Mark on the back. “You don’t have to go either,” she replied. “I can go with my girlfriends.”

“No, D, I didn’t mean it like that,” Mark responded. “I’m just trying to convince my boy Jin to come, is all.”

“What about me?” Liam cut in indignantly. “Don’t you want me to come?”

“Like I could stop you,” Mark retorted. “You’re not the one that needs convincing.”

Jin felt a sharp stab of pain. Their version of homecoming didn’t include Mina. They’d forgotten all about her, and it made him unreasonably angry at all of them. But mostly, he was upset with himself. He should be enjoying his senior year of high school. Going to prom and looking forward to starting college. He should be excited about his future. Instead, he was fixated on the life he couldn’t have. With his birth mother and with Mina. He’d spent the last few days obsessing over how he could see Mina again. The elation he’d felt at seeing her had faded into a deep fear that he’d never figure out how it had happened. He was frustrated with himself. He was reliving all the pain he’d felt the first time she disappeared. It would have been better if he’d never begun to hope in the first place.

Pushing back his seat, he excused himself to go to the restroom. He’d only taken a few steps when suddenly the brightly lit diner darkened. The loud pop music vanished. Stopping in confusion, Jin realized he was in a bar. It reeked of stale beer and vomit. He didn't recognize the strange, tinny music playing in the background.

"Hey, kid! What are you doing in here?" a burly ginger-haired bartender yelled at him.

Jin threw up his hands in apology. "Sorry, I came in by mistake." He swiftly exited the bar and stepped outside. He looked around in surprise. The area looked the same, but the street sign read RUTHERFORD WAY instead of WISCONSIN AVENUE. The neon lights of the diner were gone, and instead the storefront was all wood panel and chipped gold lettering that said MIKE'S PLACE. Next door to it was a boarded-up store that should have been a popular coffee shop. This was usually a busy area with lots of foot traffic and diners sitting outside restaurants. Instead, looking farther down the empty block, all he could see was broken glass and litter everywhere. A vagrant at the corner was sifting through an overflowing garbage can. Jin was alarmed at the state of the neighborhood.

He wondered how long he'd been in this world, but when he reached in his pocket for his cell phone, he realized he'd left it in the diner.

A car honked behind him. Jin turned to watch a few cars drive by. Something was very strange, but he didn't know what it was. All he knew was that it felt off.

"Hey, kid," a voice called from behind him. "What the hell are you doing out of school?"

Jin felt himself being spun around in a hard grip. A mean-faced man in what looked like military combat gear stood in front of him. "You're in violation of daytime curfew! All children eighteen and younger must be in school between the hours of seven a.m. and three p.m. What's your citizen ID number?"

Jin gaped in shock. "What are you talking about? I don't have a citizen ID number!"

"Are you playing with me? I can have you thrown in jail right now!"

The officer finally let go of Jin. Immediately, Jin's stomach constricted as the electrified air signaled a coming jump. He saw the shock in the officer's eyes as he disappeared.

The next moment, Jin was outside the diner, facing the busy street. He couldn't have been in the curfew place for more than a few minutes, but it had felt long and dangerous. It was definitely *not* Mina's world. He was sure of that. But he had no idea where he had just been.

What was even more troubling was what he saw in the sky. The large black swirling hole was back and bigger than ever. Jin shuddered, trying not to freak out.

From behind, he heard the jingle of a bell as a door creaked open.

"Yo, Jin!" Mark yelled. "What the heck are you doing? Your food's getting cold."

With one last glance at the ominous hole, Jin went back inside to rejoin his friends. A few minutes later, a clap of thunder startled everyone and the mood plummeted as they all watched the rain pitter-patter against the window.

"I'm gonna grab my food to go before it gets worse," Jin said. He quickly packed up his club sandwich and fries in a carryout container, paid for his meal, and left his friends behind.

The rain began to get heavier as Jin raced home. Running

up the walkway to his front door, he breathed a sigh of relief at reaching the dry shelter under the large portico. The rain pouring down all around him reminded him of the drenching he'd received when he saw Mina. Soaked through and shivering, he tried to insert his key, but strangely, it did not fit in the lock. Surprised, he rang the doorbell several times. The lights were on, and Alice was usually home during the day.

The door opened and a stranger, who looked to be of South Asian descent, appeared, holding a small dog that was barking furiously.

"Can I help you?" she asked.

Jin was confused. "Who are you?"

"Shouldn't I be asking you that?" the woman responded sharply.

Jin looked at the house number. "I'm sorry, but isn't this the Kanter residence? Dr. Phil Kanter and Alice Kanter?"

"Kanter?" the woman asked. "No. I've been living here for over a year now."

Jin just stared blankly at her, not understanding what she was saying.

"Oh, I think the family before me, the father was a doctor," she said. "Is that who you're looking for?"

Jin nodded numbly.

The woman's expression softened. "I heard that the father died and the family moved away shortly after. I'm sorry, I don't know where they went."

The woman closed her door, leaving Jin in stunned confusion. Had he stepped into Mina's world without even knowing it? Looking more carefully at his surroundings, he began to notice details he'd missed. The pretty wreath that usually hung on the door was gone. There were a bunch of artfully displayed flowerpots and a funny dog statue to the side. The welcome mat now had cute cartoon dog prints on it. Not knowing what to do, he stepped onto the walkway and stared up at the clear blue sky. At that exact moment, rain poured onto his face and Jin saw the disturbing hole in the sky outlined through the thick rain clouds. It was like a jigsaw puzzle that was missing several large pieces.

From behind him, he heard the door open again.

"Jin, what are you doing?" Alice asked. "Get in here this instant before you catch your death!"

Sheer relief sent Jin bolting into the house.

"Sorry, Mom," he said as he pulled off his dripping jacket.

"Go upstairs and get out of these wet things and I'll make you something hot and yummy to eat!"

Impulsively, Jin gave her a hug. Despite all the emotional anguish he'd been going through, he still cared deeply for his adoptive family. And he was shaken by the news the woman had given him from Mina's world.

"Ack! Jin! You're getting me all wet!" Alice laughed as she hugged him, then pushed him away. "Go on, shoo!"

Upstairs in his room, Jin's legs buckled and he sat on the floor, leaning against his door. What had just happened? He had somehow entered Mina's world, but Mina hadn't been nearby.

The woman had said the Kanters had moved away because the doctor had died. Jin couldn't believe this news. Dr. Kanter had been the one constant for Jin in both worlds. Jin couldn't imagine him not being in Mina's world. It depressed Jin to think about it.

"Come down and eat!" Alice yelled up.

Jumping to his feet, Jin quickly changed out of his wet

clothing. He still felt quivery inside as he tried to process what had just happened.

Four times now he'd been transported to another world. Three to Mina's and once to an unknown world that frightened him.

At dinner that night, Jin went up to where his adoptive father was sitting and gave him a hug.

"What's this all about?" Phil asked with a surprised laugh, awkwardly patting Jin on the shoulder.

"I'm sorry I've given you such a hard time lately," Jin said, his voice raspy with emotion. "But I want you to know I love you both. Thank you for putting up with me."

Jin sat in his seat as Alice reached over to grasp his hand, her eyes bright with unshed tears. Phil cleared his throat and grabbed Jin's other hand.

"We love you very much, and just want the best for you," Phil replied.

"We're very proud of you, Jin," Alice said.

"I know," Jin said.

"Let's eat before the food gets cold." Phil smiled.

As they ate the seafood pasta, Phil asked Jin a serious question.

"Jin, what is it you really want to do in the future?"

Surprised by the question, Jin hesitated.

"I know you applied to college as pre-med, but to be honest, I've always been a bit worried that I was swaying you to a career in medicine," Phil said. "I don't want you to be a doctor because of me. I want you to do what makes *you* happy. No one else. Just you."

Do what you feel passionate about, Mina had said. *I mean, most adults spend their lives working until they die. If you don't like your job, then life would really suck.*

Clearing his throat of the tightness that came about from thinking of Mina, Jin shrugged.

"You've always been my role model, so I thought it made sense to be like you," Jin said. "But I really don't know what I want to do anymore."

"That's what college is for. Finding out what interests you and what you want to do in the future. The choice is yours."

Jin struggled hard to contain his bitter reaction and tell Phil that he was completely wrong. Choice was an illusion. Jin had no choice in anything that had happened to him.

"You don't look like you believe me," Phil said as he peered into Jin's face.

"I'm sure it'll be fine, Dad," Jin replied.

"I'm sure you will," Phil replied.

Jin gave a perfunctory smile and pushed his pasta around his plate, hoping to change the subject.

"Oh, honey, I wanted to ask you what you wanted as a graduation present," Alice said. "Would you like something practical like sneakers or clothing or something fun?"

"Anything, Mom," Jin replied. "I'll be happy with whatever you get me."

"What do you think about a nice watch?" Phil asked with a hopeful smile. He was an avid collector of watches, especially rare, discontinued pieces, and loved talking about his collection.

For some reason, the thought of a watch made Jin remember his experience of being pulled into the curfew world without his cell phone. If he'd been wearing a watch, he would have known how long he'd been there.

"A watch would be great," Jin replied. "But I don't want you to buy me a new one. How about one of your old ones, Dad?"

Phil brightened in excitement.

"Really? You'd take one of mine?" he asked.

Jin nodded. "It would be more personal."

"Excellent! I know exactly which one to give you!" Phil jumped up from the dinner table and raced to his office.

Alice laughed at Phil's reaction. "What a wonderful idea! Your dad has always been so bummed that none of you kids had any interest in his watches. I think you just made his day!"

Jin smiled. He felt relieved and a bit guilty to see how such a small gesture on his part had made his parents really happy. Before he could respond, Phil came back to the dining room and immediately placed a beautiful stainless steel watch in Jin's hands.

"This is my old Seiko Speedtimer," Phil said. "It was the first nice watch I ever bought for myself. I got it when I was a resident and it really saved me, especially during my overnight shifts. It has a chronograph that you can use as a stopwatch. I'm sure you'll find it really useful."

"This is too special," Jin protested. "What if I break or lose it?"

"It's stainless steel and very rugged. And the value is more sentimental than monetary," Phil said. "It would mean a lot to me if you wore it."

It had a stopwatch. That was what Jin needed. "It's perfect."

"That's great!" Alice chimed in. "But it still doesn't help me come up with a good graduation present for you."

Knowing she would continue to badger him all night, Jin quickly offered up a suggestion. "I wouldn't say no to a new pair of sneakers."

"Wonderful! Let's go shopping this weekend!"

Jin agreed, but his mind was focused on the watch he was now wearing. If he teleported to Mina's or another world, he would start the stopwatch immediately without fumbling to pull out his cell phone, which might not even work.

Knowing exactly how long he was in another world was important. It was the only thing he had any control over.

CHAPTER 6

My Cosmic Love

Determined to understand what was making him teleport to other worlds, Jin thought carefully back over all that had happened to him and created a spreadsheet to document the details of each incident. He broke down what had happened:

Outside school	→ teleported to Mina's world?
Courtyard	→ teleported to Mina's world!
Diner	→ teleported to the scary curfew place
Home, front porch	→ teleported to Mina's world?

He realized that every single time he'd teleported, he'd been thinking of Mina. Even the time he ended up in the smelly bar, he'd been thinking of her. The difference that time was that he'd been angry. He remembered thinking he should never have met her, right before he ended up in the curfew place. Jin shuddered. The police officer had scared him.

But the more obvious commonality was that on the day of each teleportation, he'd seen the anomaly in the sky. It was massive and frightening and seemed to affect only him.

This had to be the answer. If only he could document it in some way. He remembered what Dr. Brennan had said.

Sometimes a thing is unexplainable. Not because it can't happen, but because we just don't know how it happens yet.

He was going to track everything and go see Dr. Brennan again. Jin thought the professor was probably his best bet for understanding what was happening. But he didn't want to bother Dr. Brennan until he had some more statistics.

Thursday, April 10

On the way to school, the first thing Jin saw was the anomaly. He was excited to see it. It had been over a week and a half since it had last been in the sky. The black hole had grown huge. It should've blocked the sun and caused darkness, but didn't. That made no scientific sense to him. But if it was something only he could see, then it wouldn't actually have the ability to cast shadows. Whatever it was, he was going to test out his hypothesis and see if it had anything to do with him teleporting to Mina's world. If he found himself in Mina's world again, he would do whatever he could to connect with her.

The school morning dragged slowly. Skipping fourth period, Jin found himself drawn to the courtyard where he'd seen Mina in the rain. He sat alone under the tree and watched as the light flowing between the leaves sent shadows dancing across the pavement. He wondered if Mina had as strong a connection to the courtyard as he did. As the thought entered his mind, he felt the uncomfortable stomach-lurching and body-shifting that signaled he'd teleported. Suddenly, he was no longer alone. He turned his head and found himself staring straight at the person he'd been thinking of.

"Mina!" Without any hesitation, Jin embraced Mina and kissed her.

"Jin, is this really you?" Mina shouted.

"I've missed you so much," Jin murmured.

"I don't understand." Mina looked him in the face. "Am I dreaming again?"

"No, I'm here, I'm really here!" Jin reached his arm around her back to quickly start the timer on his watch. "I've been here before, but never for long enough to talk to you."

"I knew I saw you! But you disappeared so fast!"

Mina cupped his face between her hands. "Are you sure this isn't a dream?" She then pinched both of his cheeks.

"Ouch! Aren't you supposed to pinch yourself?"

Mina lifted an eyebrow. "That's silly, I just need to make sure you're real."

Jin laughed and tugged at her silver-tipped hair.

"I was just sitting here, thinking of you and wishing you were here with me."

"I was wishing the same thing!" Mina said. She bounced in her seat. "Is that how it works? We have to be in the same place at the same time thinking about each other?"

"Maybe," Jin responded. "I've also been brought here without any sign of you near me."

"Wait, what does that mean?"

Jin hesitated. "I don't know. I'm trying to figure it all out."

He looked at his watch. "Also, I never teleport for too long. Possibly only a minute at most. But I've now been here for over three minutes and I'm pretty sure it's because I'm holding on to you."

Mina laughed and wrapped her arms around his neck. "Then you can't ever let me go."

He stared intensely at her. "I don't want to."

Before they could say another word, the bell rang. Soon the courtyard would be flooded with students.

"Let's get out of here!"

Holding hands, they ran through the school gates and found themselves making their way to the same park that they had sat in long ago when Mina first came to Jin's world. They collapsed onto a bench, breathless from their run.

"I still can't believe it," Mina said, staring into Jin's face. She reached up and placed her hands on his cheeks and squeezed his face hard.

"What are you doing?" Jin asked through his squished mouth.

Releasing him, she then slapped her own cheeks several times.

"Yep, I'm awake," she said with a decisive nod. She leaned her head against his chest. "You're really here!"

Jin rested his chin on the top of her head. They sat wrapped in a warm embrace until Mina faced him again.

"Tell me everything," she said. "How long can you stay? How can we meet again?"

"I'm not sure, but now that we've connected, I'm going to do some research and get some answers." Jin told Mina about meeting with Ms. Allen and Dr. Brennan.

"There must be a reason why this is happening, right? Maybe you're meant to come over here?" Mina asked.

"I don't know, but I'm planning to talk to Dr. Brennan and see if he might have any ideas."

"Do you trust him?" Mina asked.

Jin nodded immediately. "Yeah, I do. He really listened to me and took me seriously. And I liked him."

"Good! I know that talking to Ms. Allen helped me when I was in trouble over in your world," Mina said. "It's so weird that I met her whole family there, but here she's just one of the teachers at school that I know."

"So you've never talked to Ms. Allen about the webcomic?"

"Actually, it's weird. No one here connected her to Ms. A, and I don't think she ever saw it," Mina said. "But that gives me an idea . . ."

Mina chewed on her lip, her eyebrows furrowed in concentration.

"What is it?" Jin asked.

"What if we contact the version of him that is here?" Mina asked. "Two brilliant heads have got to come up with a solution, right?"

Surprised at her suggestion, Jin thought for a moment before agreeing.

"It's worth a shot." He smiled. "I mean, we can't hold hands like this forever."

Mina gripped his hand hard between hers. "But if we know how to do this, we could plan our next meeting, right? What date and time was it when you got here?"

He looked at his watch and said, "Ten-fifty a.m., fourth period, Thursday, April tenth."

"That must have been the same for me!" Mina exclaimed. "I cut out of art history early so I could come to the courtyard.

To be honest, I've been doing it a lot because I keep hoping I'll see you again. Ms. Butler hates me now. I'm probably going to fail."

Jin squeezed her hand. "She won't fail you. But it seems like our times are finally syncing up. Let's meet tomorrow, right after school."

"Can't we meet at school if we know each other's schedules?"

"Maybe, but then we risk someone seeing me teleport."

"That would be bad," Mina replied. "So what exactly do we need to do?"

"At three p.m., meet me here at that first table in the pavilion and think really hard about wanting to see me," he said. "I think we have to be close enough to touch. That's how we did it today."

Mina reached up to caress Jin's cheek. "I can't believe this is real. It feels like a miracle."

"You have no idea how much I've wanted to see you," Jin sighed.

"Me too," Mina replied.

"Are you going to prom?" Jin asked.

Mina shook her head. "I didn't want to go without you."

"Same." Jin smiled. "Although you should go with your friends. Have a good time."

"I don't want to. I'd rather sit and talk with you anywhere than go to prom without you." Mina stuck out her lower lip in an adorable pout that made Jin want to kiss her again.

"I wish I was going to prom with you."

"Me too."

Jin dropped a quick kiss on Mina's lips. "I want to hear about where you're going to college. Did you get into RISD?"

"Yes, but I decided to go to MICA instead."

"MICA?"

"Maryland Institute College of Art," Mina replied. She sat up and frowned. "How is it we both will be in Baltimore for college but in different worlds?"

There was far too much sadness in Mina's words. It hurt Jin's heart.

"That's a good thing," he remarked. "It means even when we go to college we'll be able to see each other if we plan it well."

"You really believe that?"

"Of course, look at us now." Jin pushed a stray lock of hair behind Mina's ear. "Tell me why you decided to go to MICA."

"So many good reasons! It's a great school, and they made me feel real special when they gave me a nice little scholarship. Plus, I want to be closer to home since my dad and I have been bonding a lot. He's even resorting to bribery. Said he'd bring me a week's worth of Korean food every weekend and he'll even consider getting a dog!"

"Are you still drawing webcomics?" Jin asked.

Mina shook her head with a dramatic shudder. "After what happened in your world? Hell no! Too much PTSD."

"But it was all worth it," he said. "If you hadn't created that webcomic, I would never have met you."

"It is now," Mina agreed as she leaned against his shoulder.

"I saw Aunt Jackie last week," Mina continued. "She came down for her monthly dinner with me. And she brought me this."

Mina held up a gold bangle on her arm. "She spoils me a lot," she said.

Jin flinched at hearing his mother's name.

"Wait a minute! I have something for you!" Mina hooked her lower leg around Jin's leg, reached into her backpack, and took out a magazine.

"*Vogue* did an article on Aunt Jackie and her bridal empire, as they call it," Mina said.

She opened the magazine to an article with a full-page spread of his mother smiling in her office. The caption read, *The iconic Jackie Young, whose innovative yet timeless designs of romantic whimsy have shaped the bridal fashion industry.*

"Eomma," he whispered. There were several more photos of her in her bridal salon, at her sewing machine, at her desk, and each one sent him a wave of familiarity, pain, and love. His hand trembled and his voice was unsteady. "My mom. Tell me, how is she doing?"

"She's doing great," Mina said. "But she's never stopped missing you."

The tears that he had been holding in for so long spilled over. "She looks just as I remember her."

"I have more photos on my phone if you want to see," Mina said. "When I was in your world, my phone was wiped clean of all my photos. I was sad I couldn't show you any."

Mina opened her photo library to a folder named *Aunt Jackie* and handed it to Jin. He began scrolling through hundreds of photos.

"My dad didn't get me a cell phone until I was fifteen," Mina said. "So my library only goes back a few years. But I can scan more photos to share with you."

Seeing his mother's face again filled in the missing part of his memories. Here was the mother from his childhood. The woman he had missed the most his entire life.

"She didn't leave me!" he cried.

He studied every photo and asked many questions until he felt he had caught up with all that he'd missed while he was living another life in another world.

They talked for several hours, until Mina could no longer ignore the beeping of her phone. Checking it, she sighed.

"My dad wants to know where I am and why I'm not home," she groused. She texted him back quickly as Jin kept a steady arm around her shoulders. "I'm going to have to go soon."

"I'll walk you home."

Before he could stand, Mina grabbed his backpack and placed the *Vogue* magazine in it.

"Take it, I made my dad buy ten copies of it!"

They held hands as they walked the few blocks to Mina's town house. On their way, they passed the Kanter house. Jin stopped short, remembering what the woman who now lived in the house had said.

"Mina, can you do me a favor? Can you look up Dr. Phil Kanter and find out what happened to him and his family?"

"Sure, I can do that for you."

When they arrived, Mina gripped Jin's hand. "I don't want you to go."

As Jin wrapped his arms around her body, he felt a wave of dizziness. He had to close his eyes and fight against the sudden nausea.

"Jin, you okay?" Mina asked, looking up at him.

Swallowing hard, he smiled to hide his weakness.

"Hey, maybe we should both go to prom with our friends and somehow connect if our proms are both on the same night and in the same place."

"That would be amazing!" Mina gave him a quick hug. "I

haven't been paying any attention, but I'll find out where it is and let you know!"

"Same!" Jin replied. "It would be worth all the effort if it means I could be with you at prom."

"Maybe I can find that same silver dress," she said with a grin.

"My heart!" Jin pressed his hand to his chest dramatically. "I'll see you tomorrow."

"Are you sure it will work?" Mina asked, anxious tears pooling in her eyes.

"It will, I promise."

He wanted to kiss her again, but the nausea hit him hard and his legs trembled. Just then, the front door opened.

"Mina, is that you?"

As Mina's father stepped outside, Jin let go of Mina, and he felt the lurching in the pit of his stomach as his body whisked itself back to his own world. He was standing in front of Mina's town house, but the differences were stark. The house he'd left had been brightly lit, with well-kept flowering bushes, the lawn covered with the pink petals of the familiar dogwood tree in the front yard. Here, the house was dark, the front clear of any flowers. Even the tree had not bloomed, as if it too was depressed without Mina. But the major difference was that the dizziness and nausea were gone. He felt absolutely fine again.

Jin took heart in having learned another important piece of information. Wherever he went to in Mina's world was where he returned to in his. Suddenly, he remembered the *Vogue* magazine. He quickly opened his bag and looked for it. He was both shocked and elated to find that it was still there. He checked his timer to see that he'd been in Mina's world for nearly three hours. He glanced up at the sky and was shaken to see that the hole seemed closer. As if it was slowly eating the horizon. It made him deeply uneasy. He tried to take a photo of it, but it didn't show up on his phone. He wondered if a camera with film would be able to capture it, and then he could show it to someone. Like Dr. Brennan. He needed to talk to him and tell him everything that had happened. But would the professor believe him?

Walking home, Jin was absorbed in his thoughts. He felt excited and happy for the first time in a long while. He felt hope that he'd found a way to continue to see Mina despite the impossibilities of their situation. He pushed aside the uneasy feeling that the black hole above him gave him and instead focused on the fact that he'd finally connected with Mina. He'd been able not just to talk to her, but also to hold her hand, hug her, kiss her. He'd missed her so much.

At home, his parents noticed his mood change during dinner.

"Did something happen today at school, Jin?" Alice asked with a smile. "You seem so happy."

"It's clearly because of that fine watch he's sporting on his wrist," Phil remarked. "Wearing such an elegant timepiece would make anyone proud, right, son?"

"Yes, it's the watch," Jin said. "Just looking at it makes me smile."

"What did I tell you? I'll make a watch man out of you yet!"

Jin took a bite of his pork chop and chewed. Clearing his throat, he said, "So I'm thinking I might go to prom after all."

Alice clapped her hands in delight. "Who's the lucky girl?"

A vision of Mina in her silver gown flashed before his eyes. "No dates," he replied. "Gonna go with a group of friends."

"I'm sure that will be lots of fun."

"We'll have to get you a tux!"

"I said I'm thinking about it," Jin said in alarm. "I'm not sure yet."

"Well, I'm just glad you're thinking it over," Alice said. "It will be a wonderful memory for you."

Jin noticed that he wasn't irritated with her the way he had been lately. And he knew it was because of Mina. Not just seeing her and being with her. But the gift she had given him. To see his birth mother and to know she was out there, still loving and missing him. Some of the pent-up anger he'd felt toward Alice had eased. It wasn't completely gone, but he could breathe calmly in her presence again. It was a relief. He had hated feeling angry all the time. But now, he felt hope.

His birth mom was still alive. Somehow, he would see her again.

CHAPTER 7

The Problem with the Weather

Friday, April 11

Jin woke to a text message that school was canceled due to the loss of power from the overnight storm. The morning brought heavy rain once again, more torrential downpours and flooding in many areas of the city. Jin was anxious that this would affect his ability to see Mina. All he'd dreamed about was seeing her again.

He'd also studied the article on his mother in its entirety. He remembered watching her sketch and create beautiful dresses. How she would let him run the fabric through the sewing machine. She would call him her little helper. It had both hurt and healed him to see her success. It hurt that he wasn't there with her. But it made him feel better to know that she was able to channel her grief into beauty. He was so proud of her that his heart ached.

Mark texted him, Liam, and Sam in their group chat.

Mark: im sick of all this rain.

Jin: yeah this sucks
been wanting to play
hoops

Liam: let's go to community center gym

Mark: not worth it everyone will be there
And they always lose power

Sam: my cousin works over at Silver gym
he can get us in to play
they got generators for lights

Mark: Cool what time?

Sam: 3

Liam: sweet!

Jin: I can't make 3

Mark: why not?

Jin: meeting someone

Liam: WHO
Is she hot?

Jin didn't reply and let the chat continue without him. Time seemed to be moving at snail's speed. He glared at the sky, resentful of the lousy weather. But determined to see Mina no matter how terrible it was outside.

A loud crack of thunder that seemed to reverberate right above his head made Jin nearly jump out of his skin. The weather had been profoundly bad lately, leading to doomsday videos all over social media. Small coastal towns in Florida and Texas had flooded and were practically submerged. And the other day, his parents had been watching a news report on a row of empty beach homes in the Outer Banks collapsing into the ocean.

From his bedroom window, Jin could see a wide stream coursing through the street. The rains had overwhelmed the sewer system and there was simply nowhere for all the water to go.

This catastrophic weather had intensified only recently. Ever since he began to teleport. This gave Jin pause. He wondered if there was a connection between his teleporting and the severe weather.

Jumping to his feet, Jin rummaged in his desk drawer until he found Dr. Brennan's business card. Worried that the professor would think he was delusional, Jin blanked on what to write.

> Dear Dr. Brennan, I think I know what's causing the severe weather problems. Can I come and speak with you in person? Sincerely, Jin

As soon as it was a quarter to three, Jin pulled on a raincoat and boots and headed to the park. It was completely empty. The ground muddy and unpleasant with pools of water everywhere. As horrible as the weather was, at least it allowed him to be alone. He was relieved that no witnesses would be around when he teleported to Mina's world.

Three p.m. arrived but nothing happened. Thirty minutes passed and yet he remained. He wondered if Mina had forgotten. No, there was no way she would forget. She'd been too concerned about their plan working. She would have come. She would have done everything he told her to do. Jin began to worry. What if something had happened to her? Was she okay? Twenty more minutes passed as Jin paced under the tall rafters of the pavilion. The rain had decreased in intensity.

Jin stepped away from the pavilion. The black hole wasn't in the sky. All the times he'd traveled to Mina's world, the ominous black hole had always been present. Without it, he was stuck. He had no way of letting her know the reason he wasn't with her. She was probably waiting for him. Worrying about him, not knowing what had happened. Frustrated, Jin buried his face in his hands. He'd thought this was the way he could be with Mina again. But now, he realized he was fooling himself. He couldn't ever control what happened to him. Still hoping that something would change, he sat in the park for another hour, staring at the sky. Wishing that the black hole he found so frightening would reappear because it was the only way he could see Mina. But the sky stayed cloudy and drizzly.

By five p.m., he was ready to give up. Depressed, he slowly headed home. It troubled him that Mina might have been waiting the whole time, thinking he'd forgotten or that something had happened to him. If only there was a way for him to contact her. To tell her he'd messed up.

He had walked several blocks when he felt the familiar rush of air and the queasy lurching of his stomach. He was suddenly on a dry sidewalk, the sun beaming in a cloudless sky. Pushing off his hood, he whirled around and immediately sprinted back to the park. He ran as fast as he could, so recklessly that he took a big tumble onto the street, landing hard on his knee. He jumped to his feet and limped as fast as he could. He prayed that Mina would still be there. As soon as he rounded the corner, he began shouting her name. Up ahead, he could see Mina stand up and start to run toward him.

Desperate to reach her before his time was up, Jin gritted his teeth against the pain.

"Mina, I was wrong!" he shouted. "There's one more thing that has to happen for this to work."

Before he could finish his sentence, and only inches from being able to grab her hand, Jin was pulled back to his world. He fell onto the wet grass, his palms taking the brunt of the fall. His clothing was soaked and muddy and his knee still throbbed, but it was the pain of missing Mina that hurt the most. Looking up at the sky, he saw the black hole again just as the clouds let loose another torrent of rain.

CHAPTER 8

Possibilities

Monday, April 14

Three days later, Jin was on the bus to George University. Traffic was still a mess and the Metros were closed from all the flooding. But the buses were still running, slow and steady. The thirty-minute ride took nearly an hour, but Jin finally made it to campus to meet with the professor.

"Jin, come on in!" Dr. Brennan said. "Let me finish up and I'll be right with you."

Jin wandered around the office, taking a closer look at the crowded bookcases. Very old books that ranged from philosophy and religion to science fiction were tightly packed into every crevice of the shelves. There were several detailed models of rocket ships displayed on a credenza that was also piled high with magazines and workbooks. In the far corner of the bookcase, hidden behind a stack of files, Jin caught sight of a slight shimmer on a strangely formed black rock. He stepped closer to peer at it.

"That's a meteorite and it's over a billion years old," Dr. Brennan said, walking up behind him. "It's mostly iron so it's not worth a lot of money, but it has great sentimental value to me."

He picked it up and handed it to Jin. "I found this on a family trip to Arizona, at Tonto National Monument, when I was only twelve years old. You know, if you find a meteorite on public lands it's technically federal government property. But you're allowed to keep it if it's under ten pounds, as a personal keepsake. I was obsessed with the idea that this had once been part of a massive asteroid that had hit Earth. And it was this meteorite that led me to become an astrophysicist."

Jin stared at the dense rock and wondered if the Dr. Brennan in Mina's world still had the same meteorite just sitting casually behind a stack of books in his office. Handing it back to the professor, Jin followed him to a small conference table.

"Your email was very interesting," Dr. Brennan said as he placed the rock on the table. "Why don't you sit down and tell me what you meant."

Taking a deep breath, Jin asked, "Do you remember when I told you about a recurring dream I had been having where I was waking up in another world?"

The professor nodded, intrigued.

"Well, it wasn't a dream," Jin said. "And I think every time I teleport to another world it causes the bad weather that we've been having here."

"Bad seems an understatement," Dr. Brennan responded.

"Well, yeah," Jin replied. "It's been awful."

The professor's expression changed.

"Extraordinary!" he exclaimed. "It also explains the extreme weather patterns the world has been afflicted with all at the same time."

He grabbed a globe from the bookcase and placed it on the table in front of Jin, spinning it and pointing at Asia.

"Typhoons in southeast Asia, massive blizzard in northern Russia, flooding in Europe, back-to-back hurricanes from South to North America simultaneously?" Dr. Brennan said. "It's like the movie *2012* except without the destruction of the world! Er, at least not yet, I hope?"

Jin shrugged. "I didn't see that movie, so I don't know what you're talking about."

"It's one of my favorite 'end of the world' movies, even though it's way over the top," Dr. Brennan continued. "They threw in every natural disaster possible—earthquakes, flooding, tsunamis, volcanos, you name it!"

"How does it end?" Jin asked.

"Oh, the earth is pretty much destroyed, but the main characters escape in a massive ark that was made for all the billionaires, while the rest of the people die."

Jin snorted. "That sounds about right."

Dr. Brennan stood up. He faced a large whiteboard hanging on the wall next to the table.

"This is so interesting! I feel like we're talking through the plot of an epic sci-fi movie!" Dr. Brennan rocked on his heels. "I want you to walk me through all the details."

He drew a line down the middle of the board, labeling one side A and the other B. On the A side he drew a black circle and a small stick figure and wrote *Jin*. On the

B side he drew two small stick figures and no black circle. He then proceeded to list details of what he knew of both worlds.

"You believe that you can only teleport when the black hole phenomenon is present here in A. But when you are in B, you meet Mina, and there is no black hole phenomenon there, correct?" Dr. Brennan asked.

Jin nodded.

"After each teleportation, the weather in A becomes erratic," the professor continued. He drew a tornado with an animal in the middle of it on the A side.

"Yes, but what's that?"

"The movie *Twister*! Its poster had a tornado with a cow in it," Dr. Brennan said with a smile. "I think it's so funny."

"Is there a movie you haven't seen?" Jin asked.

"Not if I can help it!" Dr. Brennan laughed.

Jin had to smile. There was something endearing about Dr. Brennan being such a movie buff.

"Can you describe the black hole phenomenon in detail for me?" Dr. Brennan asked.

Jin scrolled through some images he'd saved on his phone and showed them to the professor.

"I tried to take photos of it, but I couldn't capture it," he said. "So I did some research on black holes, and these are the images that looked most like it."

The image he passed to Dr. Brennan was one of deep space, but in the middle was a circle of utter blackness with a frayed-looking outline of blue, orange, and white light that rippled away from the center.

"It's not exact but close," Jin said. "Except the edges are

wider and the fringes look like cosmic dust. And there are all these gray clouds floating above the center."

Dr. Brennan looked at Jin in surprise. "This is a simulation of a black hole formed from a dying star. Are you sure it looks like this?"

"I think so? Is that shocking?"

"These colors would indicate that this is an active black hole. A dormant one would be harder to see with the naked eye. If this was real, our planet would be sucked into it by its massive gravitational pull and completely destroyed. We would be undergoing catastrophic climate issues."

"Kind of like what's happening now?" Jin asked.

"Much worse," Dr. Brennan replied. "We're talking tsunamis and earthquakes and whole cities vanishing. Which leads me to believe it's not a real black hole."

The professor rubbed his cheek absent-mindedly, leaving a red marker smear across his face. "If only I could see it myself."

"Do you think if I used a film camera I might capture it?" Jin asked.

"Great idea!"

Dr. Brennan walked over to open a cabinet. From a shelf, he pulled out a Nikon camera.

"Here, take this camera and try to record it," he said. "The camera on your phone might be too low-resolution to photograph it. This has one-hundred-twenty-millimeter film and can capture far more details than your phone camera. There's about sixteen frames on the roll. Use it up and bring it back to me next week. I have a darkroom where I develop all my film. I don't know if it will make any difference, but who knows."

Jin examined the expensive-looking camera. "Are you sure you want me to use something this expensive?"

"It's old and has been through the wringer," the professor replied. "But it should do the trick."

Jin thanked him and placed the camera on the table.

"Do you have any idea what that thing in the sky is?" he asked.

"Well, without seeing it myself it's hard to know. Theoretically it sounds like it could be a wormhole between two universes. That would allow for the shortest amount of time traveled. Unlike how they're depicted in movies, a wormhole would be so unstable that it would collapse the minute someone tried to pass through it."

"But I'm not actually passing through it," Jin replied. "It's just up in the sky."

Dr. Brennan rubbed his chin, getting more red marker all over his face. "Maybe you don't need to physically enter it, but somehow you spiritually pass through it."

"But I was there!" Jin exclaimed. "I held Mina's hand. I hugged her. I was in her world."

"I wish there was a way that I could go with you." Dr. Brennan sighed. "All I can give you are theories. It may be that you don't actually have to pass through the wormhole physically, it just has to be present to allow you to travel to the other world.

"Is the transition instantaneous?" Dr. Brennan asked.

"Yes, it feels immediate."

"Remember when I told you about Skybird? We're playing with a combination of quantum entanglement and tunneling that might create an actual wormhole. What if that's what you're doing?" Dr. Brennan mused.

"You think I'm quantum-tunneling?" Jin asked.

"No, you're far too big. But theoretically, it is similar. The idea that a particle can penetrate a seemingly impossible barrier and appear instantly on the other side. But it is a theory that applies at the quantum level."

Everything Dr. Brennan had said just frustrated Jin more. "So there's no explanation."

Dr. Brennan sighed. "Listen, Jin. Physics rarely has the answer. It's all about the exploration of the known unknown. This is probably why I like movies so much. Your imagination becomes alive with impossibilities. Your unique situation is a complete unknown in which I am seeking to apply untested theories to find a conclusion. I think we have to keep observing and studying, then interpreting and predicting. Every instance of your world jump is data that we must analyze. But know that all the analysis might not be correct. In fact, my mind keeps going to a theory that revolves completely around you, has no basis in the laws of physics, and is more sci-fi than science. But hypothetically, it might be the most accurate theory for your set of circumstances."

"Revolves around me? How?"

Dr. Brennan erased the whiteboard and began to draw a circle and a long line.

"Okay, hear me out. Let's call Mina's world X and this

world Y. If Y branched off from X at the moment of your death, with the sole purpose of giving you an alternate life story where you could live without any knowledge of what happened in world X, then what happens to Y when the main character becomes aware?"

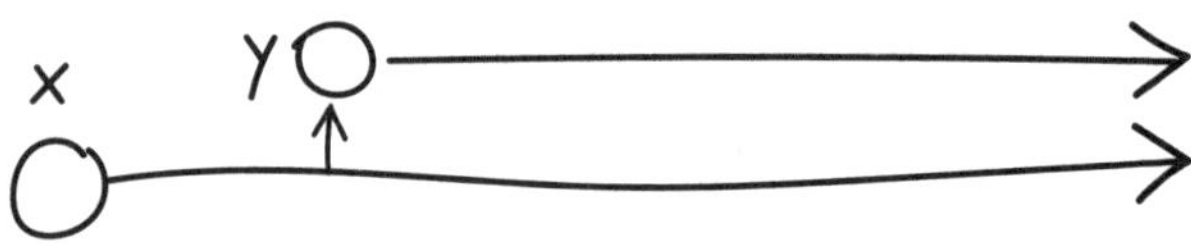

"I don't understand."

"Can Y continue to exist if it has lost its purpose? If the sole reason for its creation is gone, then Y no longer has any relevance and should be subsumed back into world X. Assuming that this world is the same except for you, then everyone in this world would be absorbed into the version of themselves that already exists in X."

The professor's words didn't immediately click.

"If this is true, then what happens to me?" Jin asked.

"Hypothetically, if there is no you there, then can you even cross over?"

"That doesn't make any sense—then why am I even traveling there? Why am I being sent to a world I can't live in?"

Dr. Brennan got visibly excited. "That's the fascinating part. Maybe the teleporting between worlds is data mining in order to find a solution to your unique situation. If this world is collapsing into the other world, and you are the only variable, then you would need to figure out how to survive what is to come."

"That's not reassuring," Jin retorted.

"And what if you aren't the only variable? What if there are children who exist here that don't exist in the other world? Once this world splits from the other, life can cause quite a lot of chaos."

"Then, if the worlds merge, they might disappear like me?"

"Possibly," the professor said.

"How can you say something so terrible in such a matter-of-fact way?" Jin asked, quite stunned.

Dr. Brennan looked horrified. "I'm so sorry, Jin. I'm not trying to be cruel. I realize that this is very real to you, while for me it's as if we're just discussing the plot of a movie."

"Well, it's not a movie, no matter how much I wish it was," Jin snapped. "I'm pretty scared by all of this."

Dr. Brennan stared at the whiteboard and then drew a stick figure on the Y timeline.

"If the instability of this world is connected to your world-hopping, then an argument could be made for the importance of you staying here and not teleporting."

"I can't control it!" Jin cried.

"Maybe you can."

"What do you mean?" Jin asked.

"There may be ways to keep you from traveling between worlds, which could allow this world to continue to exist."

His words struck fear in Jin's heart.

"You think I should not be going to Mina's world," Jin responded.

The professor shook his head. "No, I'm not saying anything of the sort. I'm merely providing another theory. The theory that if you stop teleporting, the catastrophic weather will stop and this world will remain."

Jin thought for a long moment. All these theories were terrifying and were making his head hurt.

"Question: If Mina had never come to this world and I had never found out what happened to me, would our existence here be threatened as it is?"

The professor shook his head. "It would be highly improbable. But again, this is just a theory."

Yet this theory felt very real to Jin.

"Mina would be devastated," Jin said to himself. "Thanks, Professor. I'll go now."

He stood up and walked to the door.

"Jin, at this moment, these are all just possibilities. In science, nothing is one hundred percent certain."

"That means you still don't believe me," Jin said flatly as he moved to open the door.

"That's not what I mean," the professor said. He picked up the meteorite and brought it over to Jin.

"I will tell you a secret that I've never told anyone else because it sounds too bizarre. But this meteorite *called* to me."

Jin looked at the professor in amazement, making him laugh.

"I know, right? It sounds absurd. But I heard it. Not words, but a sound. Almost musical. It sang to me and led me to this very rocky, dangerous trail that I shouldn't even have been on. I should have turned back, but I had to find what was making that otherworldly sound. And there it was, shimmering under a layer of red sand. I thought it was the most beautiful thing I'd ever seen."

Dr. Brennan placed the rock in Jin's hand. "When people ask me what made me become an astrophysicist, I answer very honestly that I was called to it. I just leave out the part that I mean it literally. The reason I'm telling you something that I've never told anyone else is because I want you to trust me when I tell you that I will help you as best I can."

Dr. Brennan took back the rock and went to put it in the bookshelf. He sat at his desk and swiftly wrote up a note, which he signed and then sealed into an envelope.

"I don't need to believe every word you tell me," he continued. "I believe that miraculous things happen every single day that make no sense scientifically. Sometimes, you have to believe with your gut over your mind. When you go to Mina's world, seek out the me that is there and give him this note. If he is me, then he will help you also."

Jin's eyes widened in surprise. Mina had suggested the same thing. Then it had to be a good idea.

Dr. Brennan handed Jin the envelope and a business card with a number handwritten on the back.

"This is my cell phone—call me if you have any questions! I always have it with me. You can text me, but my apologies if I never respond. My fingers are too clumsy for the tiny buttons. You can always email me."

"Thanks, Dr. Brennan," Jin responded. He gazed at the professor's kind face, feeling a little better. "By the way, you've got marker all over your cheek."

Dr. Brennan rubbed at his face, making the mark worse. "What else is new?" He laughed as he looked at his dirty hands. "I've always been a bit of a mess. Guess that's why I never married."

There was something sad and regretful in his tone that Jin couldn't help but notice. He wondered what the other Dr. Brennan in Mina's world would be like.

CHAPTER 9

The Portal in the Pizzeria

Monday, April 14

Jin walked to the bus stop with a heavy heart. His thoughts were caught up in what the professor had told him. If the worlds were colliding and there was no version of him in Mina's world, then he could not be absorbed into that world. But what would happen to him? Would he just vanish? Or would he appear in another world? Another reality? The idea was frightening. Horrifying. He remembered the curfew place he'd accidentally ended up in. It was depressing to realize that there was no place for him anywhere. He didn't feel like he belonged here or in Mina's world.

As the thought occurred to him, his stomach registered the rolling energy he felt whenever he teleported. Suddenly, he was standing on a broken sidewalk overgrown with tall weeds. He pressed his timer and took in his surroundings. The pristine neighborhood he'd been walking through had morphed into an area decimated by something terrible. Old buildings with broken windows and missing doors. A rustling noise startled him. Jin spun around. A doe with two fawns stared at him curiously before walking away, the fawns following on wobbly legs.

"Where am I?"

All around him nature had taken back the world. There was no sign of any humans, only the remnants of civilization. In front of him a massive tree had broken through the roof of a two-story house, its branches shoving out of all the windows. It reminded him of the Alice in Wonderland book where Alice drank the "drink me" tonic and grew so tall that her head and limbs poked out of the white rabbit's house.

A racoon ambled by him, not sparing him a passing glance, while squirrels scampered up and down the trees. There was life all around him, but no people. This world might possibly be one where all humanity was extinct. The idea was profound and heartbreaking. If he ended up here, he would die of absolute loneliness. Before the feeling could completely overwhelm him, he felt himself glitch again and he was back in his world. Relief made him feel weak. He sat on the bench within the bus shelter and took several deep breaths. His heartbeat was too rapid, he could feel it in his throat. He stopped his timer at sixty-seven seconds, and yet it had felt unbearably long.

It seemed the professor was right—there were several probabilities that could happen to him. He could possibly travel to an inhospitable world or a dangerous one. Jin shuddered. Maybe it would be best if he could find a way not to teleport anymore, but he couldn't bear the thought of never seeing Mina again.

As he sat on the bench, he spotted the swirling anomaly in the cloudy gray sky. Remembering the camera the professor had given him, Jin took several pictures of the black hole. If he was lucky, he'd finally have something to show Dr. Brennan.

Tuesday, April 15

In the morning, Jin woke up exhausted from a night filled with nightmares. He'd dreamed he was once again all alone in an apocalyptic landscape. He'd been walking farther into the abandoned neighborhood, searching for signs of human life but finding no one. He passed what once had been a supermarket, a restaurant, a bank. He kept walking until he came to a school. The front of the building was destroyed. Inside, the hallways and rooms were overgrown with vegetation. He still recognized this building. It was his high school.

As he stood there, he heard deep growling moving toward him from the depths of what had once been the school atrium. Stalking him was a pack of hungry wolves. Before he could run away, the pack charged toward him. He woke up in a sweat, relieved that he was safe in his bed. The dream had felt too real. His glitching in and out of worlds could be dangerous. And yet he was still determined to go to Mina's world.

He put the letter from Dr. Brennan and the camera into his backpack and left for school. His disturbing dreams had made him anxious to see Mina as soon as possible. Maybe he could connect with her while they were both at school. And if not, he hoped he could see her at their designated time at the park. He had decided he would go every day until they connected again. He could only hope that Mina would be doing the same.

To distract himself from his dire and intrusive thoughts, Jin went out for pizza with his friends during lunch period. The moment he entered the shop behind Mark and Sam, he felt the odd sensation of moving between worlds again, but it was as if he was stuck between them. The pizzeria looked the same, but there were completely different people inside. Mark and Sam had disappeared. Shocked, Jin stepped outside.

"What are you doing? Aren't you going in?" Liam asked over Jin's shoulder.

Jin was confused. He stood in the open doorway facing the inside of the restaurant, but he didn't see Mark or Sam. Liam gave Jin a quizzical look and pushed past him to walk inside. Jin's mouth gaped open as Liam disappeared from sight. Backing away from the pizzeria, Jin let the door slam shut. Through the glass door, he could see his friends ordering at the counter. This was something completely new.

Jin cautiously opened the door again. His friends vanished. People turned to look at him. He let go of the door and stayed outside.

After a moment, Mark popped his head outside. "Dude, aren't you coming in?"

"Not hungry," Jin replied. "I'll wait for you out here."

He looked up at the sky and realized the black hole was back and bigger than ever. Maybe Mina was inside? He entered the pizzeria and was surprised that he didn't feel any stomach upheaval or electrified air. He walked to the side, where all the tables were filled with students eating lunch. He was shocked to see people he recognized. But they gazed at him blankly. They didn't know who he was. Since Mina wasn't there, he headed outside and saw the ominous black hole floating above his head. Through the windows, he could see his friends picking up their food in paper bags and heading out. As they opened the door, Jin peered around them and once again could see the other world. It was still there. Jin didn't know what to make of it. It was as if this one spot had been caught between two different realities of itself.

The friends sat at one of the outside tables and pulled out their pizzas.

Mark shoved a paper bag into Jin's hands. "I got you a Sicilian. You're welcome."

"Thanks," Jin said gratefully.

"Sure thing," Mark replied. "You okay?"

"Yeah, why?"

"You kept opening and shutting the door, looking like you were coming inside. But then changing your mind."

"Yeah, you need to relax, Jin," Sam chimed in. "The year is practically over. No more high school!"

"Stress is clearly messing with his brain," Liam said. "I mean, is he even really Jin or is he some evil alter ego version?"

"Well, he's definitely not evil," Mark said. "More like weirdo Jin."

"I vote malfunctioning robot," Sam laughed.

"I don't know what's wrong with me," Jin admitted. "Sorry for freaking you out."

He thought of what Liam had just called him. "Hey, you guys ever wonder if there really are other versions of you living in different universes?"

"You mean like the multiverse?" Liam asked. "Hell yeah!

I'm probably like a superstar. I just haven't reached my full potential here."

Mark and Sam guffawed.

"Superstar what? Online influencer?"

"Don't laugh! That crap makes good money, dude!"

"It's not a real job," Sam remarked.

"Says you! It's a hell of a lot of work to make good content and try to get sponsorships!"

"Yeah, real hard to do goofy dances and act out stupid skits," Mark teased.

"Man, you're just jealous," Liam remarked in a peeved voice.

"They're just teasing, Liam," Jin said. "Everyone thinks your content is great. All your videos on sneakers are cool and get lots of views."

"Just not the dancing and the acting," Mark cut in with a smirk.

"But if there were many versions of you across the multiverse, would you want all of them to be social media influencers?" Jin asked.

Liam smiled. "It's what I'm good at!"

"I bet you're in jail for fraud in half of the other worlds," Sam said.

"Yeah, but I bet I was a social media influencer first," Liam retorted.

They all laughed.

"Do you think we're all friends in these other worlds?" Jin asked.

"Who knows," Mark responded. "But as long as we got to meet wherever we were, we'd be friends."

"Aw, that's so sweet." Liam batted his nonexistent eyelashes.

"You, I don't know about," Mark replied as he crumpled up his paper bag. "I think we're mortal enemies everywhere else."

"Me too," Sam agreed.

"Hey!" Liam fumed. "At least I'd have Jin."

"I think you're on your own," Jin responded. "I probably wouldn't even be in that world."

The boys all laughed, thinking Jin was joking. Jin listened and smiled as Liam launched into a litany of complaints. Being with the guys helped Jin feel less alone. These were his closest friends, who always had his back. He knew if he was in Mina's world, he'd somehow still be friends with them even if he had to find them all and start over. If he even had the chance.

Before they returned to school, Liam ran back into the pizzeria to use the bathroom. Jin followed him cautiously. This time when Liam opened the door, all Jin could see was his friend heading to the restroom. The portal to Mina's world was now gone, like it had never been there.

CHAPTER 10

The Cool Dr. Brennan

Tuesday, April 15

After school, Jin rushed over to the park and sat at the first table in the pavilion. The park was mostly empty except for some moms pushing baby strollers. He had high hopes because of what had happened at lunch and the fact that the black hole anomaly loomed above him. Anxious to meet Mina, Jin kept his eyes glued on his watch as the second hand ticked onto the twelve. Then he felt the immediate rush and the stomach-churning motion of teleportation.

"Jin!" Mina launched herself onto him before he even saw her.

"Mina! I'm so sorry." He caught her up in a tight embrace as he buried his face in her hair, breathing in her clean citrusy shampoo scent. He could have cried from the sheer relief of seeing her again.

Mina pulled away to punch him on the arm but kept a tight hold of his hand. "What happened? I was here every day waiting for you."

"In order for me to come here, there has to be a black hole in my sky. It's either a wormhole that lets me travel here or a black hole, or something like that. I don't know, I'm just glad to be here."

"A black hole? In the sky? What does that mean? Why is it happening? Did you ask that professor you were talking to?" Mina asked. "The one Ms. A introduced you to."

"That's Dr. Brennan, the astrophysics professor," Jin responded. "Yes, I've talked with him."

Jin was not going to tell her any of Dr. Brennan's theories. They were scary for him; he knew how hard Mina would take them.

"He doesn't know what it could be," Jin said. "Honestly, it might be psychological, since only I can see it."

"You're seeing it for a reason," Mina responded, her eyebrows furrowing in concern. "It must mean something."

Jin remembered what Dr. Brennan had told him.

"Mina, can you come with me now to George University? Dr. Brennan agreed with you about meeting the version of him that's in this world."

"Hey, I'm as smart as an astrophysicist!" Mina laughed as she called for a rideshare.

"So did you find out when your prom is?" Jin asked.

"It's May seventeenth at the Barrington Hotel for us, what about you?" Mina asked.

"Same! Then we're going, right?"

Mina nodded. "I'd better go dress shopping, then. But are you sure you can make it?"

Jin grinned. "As long as the black hole is there, I'll be your date!"

"What if something goes wrong?"

"Then you have a good time anyway," Jin said gently. "Let's enjoy ourselves with our friends also."

On campus, they made their way to the physics building and looked up Dr. Brennan's office. The professor had been right. He had kept the same career trajectory and ended up in the same position and even the same office.

With over an hour to kill before Dr. Brennan's office hours, Jin and Mina walked around campus.

"So this is what it would be like if we were going to college together," Jin remarked. "We'd go to class together, study together, and go on dates whenever we wanted."

Mina looked up at him wistfully. "I would have liked that."

Refusing to let the mood turn, Jin began to run, dragging Mina along.

"Hey, where are we going?"

"When we were riding here, I remember seeing a café with a big cupcake sign nearby," he replied. "Gotta feed my girl!"

The café had the biggest cupcakes they'd ever seen. They ordered a red velvet and a salted caramel, with strawberry lemonades, but when Jin went to pay, Mina swiped her card instead.

"Your card won't work here," she said. "Don't worry, I get to treat you now!"

They'd gotten into a good system of always remembering to keep in physical touch with each other. Jin carried the drinks and the box of cupcakes while Mina kept a firm grip on his arm. Sitting down on a bench, Mina hooked her foot around Jin's so they could use their hands to eat.

Mina took a huge bite of her red velvet cupcake and got cream cheese frosting on her nose.

"Why are you laughing?" she asked. "I got stuff all over my face?"

"I wish I could take a photo of you right now," he said.

She wiped her mouth and checked her face on her phone before grabbing her Polaroid camera from her bag.

"When I returned home from being in your world, I was really depressed that I didn't even have a picture of you. But then I found our homecoming dinner Polaroid in my bag, and it helped me know that I hadn't imagined you."

She snapped two selfies of them and then a photo of Jin alone. Spreading a napkin on the bench between them, she set the Polaroids down and then passed the camera to Jin. Excited to have a photo of Mina right away, Jin carefully aimed and took the picture. Mina placed the Polaroid next to the first one. When Jin tried to sneak a peek, Mina slapped his hand gently.

"No peeking! Leave it for ten minutes."

After they'd eaten the sweets and finished their drinks, the Polaroids were ready. Mina crowed happily over their photos and tucked two into her fanny pack. Jin wasn't ready to put his away. Mina looked so pretty with her big smile and the smattering of freckles across her nose and cheeks.

"These are my only photos of you," Jin said. "All the ones I took on my phone disappeared when you left."

He was glad to have them, but it wasn't enough. He wanted more than a photo. He wanted Mina and his old life.

He wanted to see his birth mother. A pang of grief caused him to tear up. He didn't want to go back to his world.

"I'll tell you what, every day we're together we can take another Polaroid," Mina said.

He placed his treasures carefully in his wallet.

"Now, tell me about you. How is Jin? How are you dealing with all that's happening to you?"

This was why he loved her so much. She saw him. All of him. And cared.

"I'm always great when I see you," Jin answered as he dropped a kiss on her lips.

"And?" Mina asked.

"And . . . it's been really hard," he admitted. "After you left, I was angry at everyone, especially at Alice. I know she didn't deserve it. I shouldn't resent her. It's not her fault that I got separated from my birth mom, and yet I couldn't seem to help myself. Because I want to see her, my birth mom. I want to see her so bad it hurts. But I'm scared. Just in case it doesn't work out."

"Jin . . ." Mina squeezed his hand tightly.

"I'm okay. It's just really confusing," he continued. "Which made me bitter and resentful and I had a hard time controlling my emotions and I've been a jerk to everyone."

"You a jerk? I don't believe it!" Mina smiled.

"That's because you don't see it. I was terrible! But things are better now," Jin replied. "Lots of therapy. For all of us!"

Mina's smile faded as she took a folded piece of paper out of her bag and passed it to him.

"Jin, I researched the Kanters for you," she said.

Opening the paper, Jin saw that it was a printed copy of a news article.

> **Beloved pediatric oncologist Dr. Philip Joseph Kanter passed away on October 27 of this year, when he fell from a ladder and struck his head. He'd been trying to remove an empty bird's nest over his porch roof when he lost his balance.**

He had died two years ago. Jin couldn't bear to read any more and put it away. "Did you find out about the rest of the family?"

"Apparently Alice Kanter and her two daughters moved to Boston, where her family is," Mina said. "I'm sorry."

Jin was quiet for a long moment. "It's just hard to know that you and Mom can't be with me in my world and my adopted family isn't here in this world. I guess life is just unfair."

Standing up, Mina pulled him to his feet. "Let's go see the astrophysicist now."

When Jin stood up, a wave of dizziness nearly overcame him. He swayed on his feet for a moment.

"What's the matter?" Mina stared at him anxiously as she gripped his hand. "You look pale, are you okay?"

After a moment, the dizziness passed, but Jin felt tired. As if he hadn't slept all night and was trying to force himself to keep awake.

"I'm fine," he reassured Mina. "I just got dizzy."

They returned to the physics building and knocked on the office door. They entered to see the professor staring up at them in surprise. At first, Jin marveled at seeing someone identical to the Dr. Brennan who had sent him here in the first place. He even had the same warm gaze. But Jin immediately noticed so many differences. This Dr. Brennan was dressed fashionably. Instead of old-fashioned horn-rimmed glasses, this professor wore modern clear-framed glasses. His salt-and-pepper hair was short, and his entire appearance was crisp and neat. Jin couldn't imagine him with marker smeared all over his face.

"May I help you?" the professor asked.

"Hi, Dr. Brennan," Jin said. "I have a really outrageous story to tell you, but first I'm supposed to give you this letter to read."

Dr. Brennan took the envelope and examined it. He peered sharply at Jin.

"Is this some kind of joke?" he asked.

"No, I promise you this is a serious matter that I need your help with. I'll explain everything after you read this."

Jin and Mina watched the professor as he read the letter. When he was done, he looked at them both with a neutral expression.

"So now tell me your story," he said in a measured tone.

Before Jin could say anything, Mina began to speak.

"It's all my fault," she said. "I created a webcomic that connected our worlds."

Jin listened as Mina not only explained what had happened when she entered his reality, but also explained all that he'd told her. It was as if she knew he was feeling ill. When she faltered, Jin mustered up the energy to explain the black hole anomaly and teleporting and the conversations he'd had with his Dr. Brennan, until he was too tired to keep talking. Mina squeezed his hand and searched his face in concern.

"Are you okay?" she asked.

Jin nodded and gave her a small smile of reassurance.

He was a bit rattled by Dr. Brennan's nonreaction as he continued to stare at them with an expressionless face.

"So, I am to believe that this is a letter from myself in another world, as well as to believe everything you've told me. I will be frank, I do not believe any of it."

"Excuse me, but don't you recognize your own handwriting?" Mina asked in an accusatory tone.

"Maybe you are both excellent forgers."

Before Mina could argue, Jin pointed to the meteorite in the bookshelf. Unlike Dr. Brennan in Jin's world, this Dr. Brennan had placed the rock in a glass display case.

"My Dr. Brennan told me an interesting secret about that rock," Jin said. "One that he has never told anyone. He, I mean you, found that meteorite in Tonto National Monument when you were twelve. And it is the reason you became an astrophysicist."

Dr. Brennan waved dismissively. "That's not a secret, I tell that story in every interview."

"You told me that the only reason you found the rock was because it sang to you. That it was the most beautiful otherworldly sound you'd ever heard. It called to you."

For the first time, Dr. Brennan was visibly surprised.

"He was wrong about one thing—I told that secret to only one other person," he said. "I don't know how you learned this, but it still doesn't prove you are from another world."

Jin sighed. His body ached and he could barely stay awake. But he knew what he had to do. He gave Mina a soft kiss. "I'll see you soon, I promise."

Mina hugged him. "I'll be at the park every day."

Jin looked back at Dr. Brennan. "Hopefully this will help

you believe." He let go of Mina's hand and teleported back to his reality.

Dr. Brennan jumped and let out a loud curse when Jin appeared in the chair in front of his desk.

"Jin! How the hell did you do that?"

Jin blinked and stretched. The exhaustion that he'd been feeling had dissipated. He felt completely fine again. He wondered if it was related to staying in Mina's world for longer periods.

Dr. Brennan's horrified surprise made Jin laugh. "I just saw the other you in Mina's world. I gave him your letter, but he refused to believe me. I had no choice but to let go of Mina's hand in front of him, and here I am. I thought that might shock him into believing me."

Dr. Brennan put a hand to his chest.

"Please don't do that again," he said. "You nearly gave me a heart attack. If I hadn't seen you appear before me out of thin air with my own eyes, I wouldn't have believed it myself."

Jin grinned. "Yeah, the other you probably has the same expression that you have right now."

Dr. Brennan gazed at Jin with awed wonder. His messy hair and wrinkled shirt were reassuringly familiar to Jin, especially after the reserve of the other professor.

"Tell me, what does it feel like?" Dr. Brennan asked.

Jin thought about it for a moment. "Do you know those drop tower rides at the amusement park where you plummet to the ground and your stomach jumps into your mouth? That's what it feels like."

The professor had taken out a memo pad and was writing furiously on it.

"How long does that sensation last?"

"Only a few seconds."

"What else happens when you jump to another world?"

As Jin answered Dr. Brennan's rapid-fire questions, it dawned on him that the professor was taking him seriously. Although Dr. Brennan had always said he believed him, this was the first time Jin truly felt it.

"When do you see Mina again?"

"As long as the black hole is in the sky, I'm to meet her at three p.m. tomorrow."

"And were you able to take pictures of the black hole phenomenon?"

"Oh yes," Jin answered as he took the camera out of his backpack. "I tried my best."

"Terrific! I'll develop them so we can see what you were able to capture." Dr. Brennan placed the camera in his desk drawer. "What was it like talking to the other me?"

"You were definitely a lot more suspicious and disbelieving," Jin replied.

"Of course! It is a truly unbelievable story. But I'm sure the next time you go back to the other me's office it will be different. I'm sure he—or I, who is he—will have a lot of questions and hopefully some correspondence for this me," Dr. Brennan said. He was both flustered and pumped up.

"Okay," Jin replied. "But do you really think this is going to help?"

"I really hope so," Dr. Brennan responded earnestly. "I want to take it back to my team. That way we can get more people thinking about this extraordinary development!"

“Team?” Jin asked in surprise. “You’re going to tell them about me?”

“Of course!” Dr. Brennan said. “My team at Tundra Labs are some of the smartest people in the world. They’re going to be blown away by all of this!”

An anxious feeling struck Jin when he heard the professor’s words, but he brushed it off. He needed all the help he could get.

CHAPTER 11

He's Radioactive

Wednesday, April 16

Jin woke up to hurricane winds so powerful, all the windows of his house seemed to shake. Alarmed, he ran downstairs. His parents sat in the kitchen drinking coffee and watching the news.

"Good morning, Jin," Phil said. "You're up early. But no need! They canceled school due to the terrible weather. Lucky you."

"This is not lucky, Phil!" Alice retorted. "Jin, the roads are so dangerous right now even your father closed his office. And you know he never closes his office!"

At that moment, a loud crash came from the street. Jin and his parents raced to the front windows of the living room. They all saw that a large tree had fallen on top of several parked cars.

"My gosh, that was close," Phil said. "If that tree had fallen a little to the left it would have hit us."

"None of us are leaving the house today," Alice said. "It's too dangerous! Jin, do you want breakfast or are you going back to sleep?"

"I'm going back to bed," he responded. But he stayed glued to the window even after his parents returned to the kitchen. He couldn't see the black hole in the sky. All he saw were the thick and angry-looking storm clouds that poured heavy sheets of rain.

By the afternoon, the winds died down, the rain stopped, and the sun was shining. Jin had been counting the minutes. At 2:45 p.m., he dashed out of the house.

He dodged around the massive tree that had fallen in front of their house. The sidewalks were littered with branches and debris. Traffic was a snarled mess due to accidents everywhere. The park looked completely different. A tree had crashed on the pavilion roof. Now there was yellow tape surrounding the entire area, right where Jin needed to meet Mina. The bigger problem for Jin was that the skies above him were completely clear. There was no black hole in sight.

Three p.m. came and went. Jin was still at his park. By five-thirty, he knew it was hopeless. Mina couldn't be waiting any longer. He walked home slowly, worrying about the connection between the terrible weather and the black hole. Dr. Brennan had said that a real black hole would have caused catastrophic damage to the planet. The volatile weather was the number one topic on every news program. Meteorologists from around the world were weighing in on the severity of the effects of climate change. Record heat, record cold, record rain, record wind, record flooding, record wildfires. They were breaking records on almost everything. Jin wondered if the severity of the weather was related to how long he stayed in Mina's world. He didn't want to ask the professor because he was scared of the answer, but he texted him anyway.

The professor called a minute later.

"Jin, tell me what's going on. You were unable to teleport to Mina's world because the observed anomaly was not present?"

"Yeah, it was there all night but I haven't seen it since six this morning."

"Interesting," Dr. Brennan remarked. "I was going to tell you when I saw you, but I think you were able to capture part of the phenomenon on film. I know it's hard to get around town right now, but as soon as you can, please come to campus before you try to teleport again. And bring the same clothing and shoes that you wore the day you last teleported."

"Okay, but why?"

"If it's true that your travel is causing the severe weather patterns, we need more information to gauge the impact. And I want to check something on items that you were wearing."

"Even if they've been washed?"

"Doesn't matter, just bring them."

"I'll come as soon as I can," Jin replied.

But it was several days before Jin could make the trek back to campus.

Friday, April 18

On Friday, Jin skipped school to meet with Dr. Brennan.

"Jin, I'm glad you're here," Dr. Brennan said as he waved him toward a chair. "Did you bring your clothing?"

Jin passed a bag with his jeans and sweatshirt to the professor.

"I'm wearing the same shoes," he said. "But why did you need them?"

"After you appeared in my office, I decided to test for radiation exposure," the professor explained.

"I borrowed this personal radiation detector counter from the Department of Nuclear Engineering so I could test the chair you were sitting on for radiation." Dr. Brennan pointed to a small yellow gadget with a screen and a black radioactive symbol on it.

Jin was confused. "What for?"

"If you're jumping from one world to another, you're subjecting yourself to cosmic radiation without the protection of the earth's atmosphere and magnetic field," Dr. Brennan replied. "The last time you were here, I borrowed a Geiger counter, and while radiation does dissipate, it still gave an approximate reading of six millisieverts of radiation."

"Is that a lot?" Jin asked.

"Don't worry! It's not enough to turn you into the Incredible Hulk," the professor said. "It's about how much radiation you'd get from a CT scan. One time isn't dangerous, but repeated jumps could be. That's why I wanted you to come by so I could do a reading on you. Space radiation is a concern. For example, the moon has about two hundred times the radiation levels of Earth. Who knows how much your body is subjected to each time you teleport."

Dr. Brennan picked up the gadget and stood up. "Let's start by testing you out. Would you mind standing up?"

Unnerved by the professor's words, Jin stood by the back wall as Dr. Brennan pulled on heavy gloves and turned on the detector, which immediately began to make a series of clicking sounds.

"This personal detector is more accurate for measuring how much radiation you might have absorbed," Dr. Brennan said as he ran the device close to Jin's body, starting with his head.

The little gadget let out a rapid flurry of clicking noises that seemed loudest near Jin's feet.

"Curious," Dr. Brennan said. "Would you mind taking off your sneakers and moving away from them?"

When Jin had stepped several feet away from his shoes, the professor ran the detector across his body once again, but the clicks were normal and muted. Only when it came close to his shoes were the alarming rapid-fire clicks set off again.

"Wow! Would you look at that?" Dr. Brennan said with a loud whistle. "All the radiation seems to have been absorbed by your shoes!"

The professor scratched his head, perplexed. "The first reading was quite high at ten millisieverts, but it looks like it's already dropped down to nine in the second reading."

"Why is that?" Jin asked.

"Well, in all likelihood, the radiation is dissipating, but at what rate?"

After testing the sneakers, the bag of clothing, and then Jin once again, Dr. Brennan asked, "Can you leave your shoes with me?"

"But what do I wear home?" Jin asked.

"Lucky for you, there's a shoe store nearby, which means you get a new pair of sneakers on me!" Dr. Brennan said. "Just let me know your size. I'll run over right now. I promise not to be too cheap."

Jin agreed in bemusement and watched as the professor carefully put his sneakers in a large silver padded bag.

"To be safe, I think we need to do a complete health exam to see what effects the teleportation is having on your body."

"Do I have to?" Jin asked.

"It would make me feel a lot better if we could go to the university hospital and run a gamut of tests," the professor said. "Radiation poisoning doesn't always present itself right away."

Jin hated hospitals, but he reluctantly nodded. Once again, he felt an uneasiness that he couldn't explain, even though he trusted Dr. Brennan. Something in his gut was sending a warning signal.

"While I'm gone, I'm going to give you a little assignment. Please write down each time you teleported, when the severe weather occurred, and how long the weather pattern lasted," Dr. Brennan said as he passed Jin a notepad and pencil. "I'll be right back."

Jin watched the professor leave the office. He was glad that he'd been wearing his older sneakers because of the weather. With a sigh, he sat down at the conference table and charted out all the details of his trips to Mina's world. Just when Jin was beginning to wonder what was taking so long, Dr. Brennan returned with another man.

"Jin, I want to introduce you to my Tundra Labs colleague Dr. Vance," Dr. Brennan said. "He just *happened* to be on campus today. When I mentioned you were here, he volunteered to come give you a health check and some blood tests."

Jin couldn't help but notice the questioning look Dr. Brennan gave Dr. Vance, as if he wasn't quite sure why the other man had followed him to his office. Jin's uneasiness heightened.

Dr. Vance was a stern-looking older white man with a neatly trimmed ducktail beard that didn't cover his flabby jowls. He nodded briefly at Jin and handed him a business card that read: DR. MARTIN VANCE, DIRECTOR OF DIAGNOSTIC RADIOLOGY AND NUCLEAR MEDICINE, TUNDRA LABS. There was something deeply off-putting about this man. If Jin had to pinpoint why, it would be the coldness of his small blue eyes and the deep-set wrinkles that pulled his fleshy lips into a perpetual frown. He was dressed in a blue suit with a white dress shirt and a navy-blue tie with gold stripes. Jin could see the disdain in Dr. Vance's eyes when he looked at Dr. Brennan in his stained, rumpled shirt and baggy pants.

"I thought I was going to the university hospital?" Jin asked.

"There's no time to waste. It would be best to rule out any possible radiation poisoning," Dr. Vance answered. "And I'm more experienced than any hospital staff, as I run these tests on my own employees to check their radiation levels weekly."

"I think I'd rather wait and talk to my dad," Jin said.

"Don't be a fool," Dr. Vance snapped. "I'm here right now."

Angered by Dr. Vance's arrogance, Jin wanted to refuse.

But then he noticed the sharp glare Dr. Vance gave Dr. Brennan.

"That is true," Dr. Brennan said in a conciliatory tone. "At least this will save you a trip to the hospital."

Since he trusted Dr. Brennan, Jin let Dr. Vance run several tests with machines that Jin was unfamiliar with. When Jin asked how much blood they needed, Dr. Vance ignored him. It was Dr. Brennan who explained they would need at least three vials of blood for accurate testing. Dr. Vance missed Jin's vein twice.

"He's dehydrated," Dr. Vance barked at Dr. Brennan. "I'm going to have to go through his hand."

Jin didn't like Vance's tone.

"It's not Dr. Brennan's fault. I thought you said you were good at this?" Jin snarked as the doctor painfully jabbed him in the hand. Blood flowed slowly, but not once did the doctor apologize for hurting Jin.

Jin was relieved when it was all over. He didn't like the doctor at all.

"When will we have the results?" Dr. Brennan asked as the other man prepared to leave.

"In two days," Dr. Vance responded curtly. With a brusque nod, he left.

"What a jerk," Jin said when they were alone. "And he's really rude to you."

Dr. Brennan sighed. "I'm sorry about that. Dr. Vance is pretty high up at Tundra. I can't really say no to him when he offers to help us."

Jin nodded. Dr. Vance had made it very clear that he outranked the professor. It made Jin despise him even more.

“Here are your shoes,” Dr. Brennan said as he handed Jin a bright orange box with a famous logo across the top.

“Oh, wow, these are much more expensive than the shoes you took from me,” Jin remarked in surprise.

The professor smiled. “Courtesy of Tundra Labs,” he said. “I let Dr. Vance pay for them, since he was taking your shoes to the lab to test also. And they can definitely afford them.”

As he put on the fancy new sneakers, Jin couldn’t help but worry that there was a catch to taking them. Pushing the thought aside, he thanked Dr. Brennan and left to go home.

CHAPTER 12

Two Professors Are Better than One

Monday, April 21

Jin spent the entire weekend staring up at the sky, waiting to see the anomaly that would allow him to be with Mina again. It wasn't until Monday at lunch that he spotted it.

After school, Jin turned down his friends' request to play ball and booked it over to the park once again. The tree that had crashed down on the pavilion was gone, but the roof still had a big hole and the tables had been removed.

This time, right at three p.m., he was immediately pulled into Mina's world. Once again, Mina launched herself into Jin's arms as soon as she saw him.

"All my friends think I'm crazy to sit in the park for hours every single day, but it's all worth it when I get to see you!"

"Same," Jin said. "I feel like I'm living for these moments."

He swooped her up for a kiss that left them both breathless.

"Enough." Mina hit him lightly on the chest. "We're in public. Behave yourself."

"Yes, ma'am," Jin replied. "What happened with Dr. Brennan when I disappeared?"

Mina laughed. "I wish you could have seen it! Poor guy! He was so confused! You know how his face was like a total poker face the whole time we were talking to him?"

Jin nodded. "He didn't believe us at all."

"Well, when you disappeared, he snatched his glasses off and stared at them as if they were broken! And then he came over and picked up your chair to look under it. He made me stand up and he looked under my chair as well. It was hysterical!"

"Did he say anything?"

"He kept asking me to tell you to come back and I was like 'I can't! You have to wait until the next time he teleports.' And he paced back and forth and was studying all the walls of the room as if we'd installed a trapdoor or something in his office. He even went out into the hall. He was just in complete shock."

"So he believes us now?"

"Yeah, I think so. He questioned me for fifteen minutes straight and asked me when I would be bringing you back. He gave me his number so we can contact him."

"Should we go see him now?"

"Um, can we go cat first? I'm hungry," Mina said sheepishly.

Jin grinned and leaned down to kiss her on the tip of her nose. "Of course! Where do you want to go?"

"There's a gyro place that I've always wanted to try." Mina started pulling Jin toward the street.

"How about we text Dr. Brennan and let him know we'll come by at five?"

"Great idea!" Mina laced her fingers through Jin's. "The bus goes straight to the gyro place, and then we can walk off the food as we head to campus."

Laughing at his girlfriend's delighted expression, Jin couldn't help but ruffle her hair.

"Do you have a death wish?" she growled.

They enjoyed the bus ride, spending the time talking so much that they nearly missed their stop. Jin appreciated the subtle but firm manner in which Mina made sure to always be in contact with him, even when he would forget. Like when he helped carry a baby stroller onto the bus, Mina discreetly laid a hand on his back as if to push him up. When he carried the tray of food back to their table, she grabbed his belt loop. Instead of sitting across from him, she slid into the booth next to him and tucked her foot around his.

Mina held on to Jin's waist as he pulled his backpack on.

"What do you think would happen if you didn't have your backpack on when I let go?" Mina asked. "Do you think it would stay here?"

"Probably?" Jin responded. "I tell you what, we'll test it out with something else next time."

"That reminds me! I promised we'd take a picture every time we meet," Mina said.

After taking several Polaroids, they walked to the campus. Mina chattered about school and college and everything under the sun. When she finally paused, Jin stopped to look her in the face.

"Mina, it's okay," he said.

"What are you talking about?"

"You're nervous about what the professor is going to say. So am I. We can talk about it. You can be honest with me. We shouldn't avoid the topic."

At his words, Mina deflated like a balloon.

"I'm just worried." She heaved a deep sigh. "I'm afraid you'll disappear at any moment and I won't see you again. I want to hold on to you forever, but I know I can't. And what if I have to go to the bathroom at some really important moment?"

"I promise I won't make you go to the bathroom in front of me." Jin laughed.

"No, I'm serious! Everything that's happened to you is all my fault! All these problems in your world, the world-jumping! Now I'm the only one holding you to this one. And you need help, and what if I mess up again?"

Jin hugged her. "You've already been a bigger help and support to me than you'll ever know. I'm grateful to have you."

"I'm just scared of losing you again." Mina's voice quivered with the tears she was trying to suppress.

"It's not going to happen, that's why we're going to see Dr. Brennan, remember? He's going to help," Jin reminded her.

Rubbing her eyes, Mina nodded. "Come on, it's almost five and we still have to get to campus."

By the time they reached Dr. Brennan's office, Jin was more tired than Mina. He looked at his watch and saw that after two hours in Mina's world, his exhaustion began.

At Dr. Brennan's office, the door was swung open by a brightly smiling Black woman in a perfectly tailored suit, with her hair up in a tight bun.

"You must be Jin and Mina. I am Dr. Chandra Prescott," she said, shaking their hands. She then pointed to Dr. Brennan, who was seated behind his desk. "And you know my husband, Dr. Albert Brennan."

The professor stood up and came over to shake their hands warmly, a very different welcome from their last experience. Once again Jin couldn't help but compare him to the other Dr. Brennan. This professor wore a neatly pressed lilac button-up shirt with a vivid purple tie and dark gray slacks. He had a bit of a swagger and polish that the other Dr. Brennan lacked.

Bet he *wouldn't let Dr. Vance walk all over him like the other Dr. Brennan did,* Jin thought.

"Come sit at the table," Dr. Brennan said.

Jin and Mina sat close together across from Dr. Brennan and Dr. Prescott, still surprised by their reception.

"You must be wondering what I'm doing here," Dr. Prescott said. She passed them her business card, on which her title was listed as Professor of Theoretical Physics at Atlantic University, the other prestigious college in the city. "After meeting you, Al came home in an absolute state of shock. He showed me your letter and told me you've been teleporting between two different but similar realities. I specialize in creating theoretical and computational methods to study black holes, so as you can imagine, I was blown away by your story and insisted that I be present if and when you both returned."

Dr. Prescott radiated a warmth that was palpable. Right away Jin found himself liking her and wanting to trust her.

"Remember when I told you that I had told my secret to one person? That was my wife," Dr. Brennan said, his face aglow with pride. "The fact that the other me told no one made me realize that there was one major difference between us. I had married Chandra and he had not. But tell me, how different are we?"

"Well, he's more like the absent-minded professor type," Jin replied.

Dr. Prescott started to laugh. "That's what he was like when I first met him. All rumpled shirts and messy hair. But fortunately, he cleaned up very nice."

"He must be single, then," Dr. Brennan said. He sighed when Jin nodded.

"It must have been because of our first date," Dr. Prescott said. "It was kind of a disaster."

"Everything that could go wrong, did." Dr. Brennan smiled lovingly at his wife.

"Albert had come down from Boston for a conference that he was speaking at," Dr. Prescott explained to Jin and Mina. "We met and he asked me to dinner. I suggested Anna's Café, which was a pretty popular place near his hotel. But Al, not knowing the area too well, went to Café Anne's, which was on the other side of town. So we both sat and waited for a while and thought we got stood up.

"It wasn't until the last day of the conference that we bumped into each other in the elevator. He was heading to the airport and I was going home and I let him have it."

"She really did yell at me for standing her up." Dr. Brennan chuckled. "And then she got off the elevator in a huff."

"I was mad." Dr. Prescott reached over to pat her husband's hand.

"And that must have been the moment when the other me and I diverged, because I remember I had a split second to react. Stay on the elevator and ride down to the garage where I'd parked my rental car to go to the airport, or get off and chase after this brilliant, beautiful but angry woman. I got off just as the doors began to close and I caught up with her and begged her to give me another chance. I ended up missing my flight but had the best first date of my life."

"So the Dr. Brennan in my world stayed on the elevator and caught his flight," Jin mused.

"Frankly, I'm surprised he did," Dr. Brennan said. "Right when Chandra stepped off, there was a power surge, and the lights flickered. I saw it as a sign from above not to let this woman go."

"Wait a minute, you mean if the lights hadn't flickered you wouldn't have gone after me?" Dr. Prescott asked.

"Honey, I was already out the door after you, lights or no lights!"

Dr. Prescott gave her husband a massive side-eye before turning back to Jin and Mina.

"Well, that was over eleven years ago," she said. "And we celebrate our tenth wedding anniversary this summer."

"Eleven years ago!" Mina exclaimed. "That was when Jin died in this world. On June fifteenth."

The two professors looked at each other in shock. "That was when we had our do-over dinner date," Dr. Brennan said. "I wonder how different you and I are over there."

"Well, that's not important right now—they are," Dr. Prescott said, pointing at Jin and Mina.

"Right, so the reason my wife is here is because her research is in dark matter and black holes," Dr. Brennan said proudly. "She's been dying to meet you."

"To be honest, if I didn't trust my husband, I would not have believed this was possible," Dr. Prescott responded. "Mina, could we see the webcomic that started it all?"

As Mina took out her tablet and showed the two professors her webcomic, Jin explained about the other Brennan's theories and what had been happening with the weather and the now massive hole that appeared before he could travel between worlds.

"Jin, I would really love to see those photos you took," Dr. Brennan said. "Was there anything that the other me told you that you haven't shared? It'll be important for both of us to work with the same set of information and also understand what we are both thinking."

Jin hesitated. How could he mention the professor's theory that all of this was Mina's fault?

"It is imperative that we share all information—don't leave anything out."

Holding Mina's hand tightly, Jin slowly began to relate what the other Dr. Brennan had outlined.

"Since he was sure it wasn't an actual black hole, he mentioned things like tunneling and wormholes," Jin explained. "The only real theory was the wildest one, more science fiction than science, but the one he thought was most true."

"That's okay, physics can be a little like the Wild West in terms of theories," Dr. Prescott said.

"He said the theory revolves around me as the main character in a world that branched off from Mina's world solely for the purpose of keeping me alive. But if the only reason for its creation is gone, then that other world no longer has any relevance and will merge back into the original world."

"Theoretically, in order for that to be true, everyone in the second world must have a version of themselves already existing in the original one," Dr. Prescott said.

"Except Jin," Mina whispered. "He died here."

Jin could see where Mina's thoughts were heading, full of guilt and blame.

"Dr. Brennan thinks that what's happening to me might be a way of trying to help me find my place here."

"But this is all my fault." Mina's free hand was pinching and pulling at the hem of her shirt. "If I hadn't created that webcomic, then Jin would be living his life there with no danger. Everything's all my fault."

Dr. Prescott reached over to grab both Jin's and Mina's free hands.

"Jin, if the worlds are truly colliding, then we must figure out what we need to do to bring you over safely," she said. "Mina, there is no right or wrong. Life happens, whether through the application of your webcomic or some other event. Who is to say something far worse wouldn't have occurred? What if it was the other way around and our world was colliding with Jin's? Then you, Mina, would be the one we'd be trying to help come over. But one thing we know for certain. We are in the realm of the impossible being possible."

"Does that mean you can help us?" Jin asked.

"Yes, we're going to be looking into this," Dr. Prescott said.

Relief made Jin lightheaded. "Okay, I should go see the other Dr. Brennan now," he said. He went to stand up and felt the blood rushing to his head. His knees buckled and his eyes went dark. He would have fallen if Mina hadn't been gripping his arm.

"Jin! What's the matter?" Mina asked.

Jin slumped into his chair. He began to sweat profusely as he fought off a wave of nausea.

"Jin, has this happened before?" Dr. Brennan asked.

Without opening his eyes, Jin nodded. "Last time I was here, but not this bad," he whispered.

"Then you have to go back now," Dr. Brennan said. "I've written a response to the other me. Basically, affirming what has happened and hoping we can share information that could help you. I'm going to place it in your backpack. And then you can go home."

Jin cracked open his eyes. "Thank you," he said.

And with that, he let go of Mina's hand.

CHAPTER 13

Stuck Between Two Bookstores

Monday, April 21

Dr. Brennan's office was empty when Jin arrived. He looked at his watch and saw that it was after seven p.m. It looked as if the professor had left for the night. Just like last time, Jin took note that the sickness he'd felt was entirely gone once he was back in his world. The thought was disturbing, but he pushed it aside.

Jin was moving to place the envelope from the other Dr. Brennan on the desk when he noticed a pile of photos with a note on top of a file folder.

> Jin, these are duplicates for you. Share them with the other me.—Dr. Brennan

At the very top was a picture of the blue sky with a darkened, shadowy circle in the middle. The next ten photos were close-ups of the circle. They looked grainy, with spots of blackness.

He wrote a note to the professor thanking him and stuck the photos in his backpack. He was going to leave the note on top of the file folder when he realized that it had his name on it. The normally messy desk had been completely cleared off but for the one folder placed at the center of the desk with papers fanning out of it, as if Jin was meant to see it. Curious, he picked up the papers, which looked like the lab results from his blood tests. Across the top in red letters, it was marked CONFIDENTIAL. He didn't understand what the numbers referenced, but the typed notes on the last page unnerved him.

> **No radiation detected but irregular blood count with elevated white and red blood cells. Possible abnormal DNA markers. Need further testing. Bring subject to TULLY immediately.**

It was signed by Dr. Martin Vance. Alarm bells were going off in Jin's head. Why the hell was that creepy doctor demanding that he be taken to TULLY? He vaguely remembered Dr. Brennan telling him that it was a Tundra lab four thousand feet underground. But he didn't understand why he would have to go all the way there just for testing. The thought of such a deep-underground lab made Jin claustrophobic. There was no way he'd go. But it was the demand that Dr. Brennan bring Jin immediately that troubled him the most. Vance was Dr. Brennan's higher-up. Jin left the letter from the other Dr. Brennan on the file and hurried out of the office.

The sky was completely dark and drizzling as Jin ran across campus. By the time he reached the bus stop, the drizzle had turned into a steady, heavy rain. The temperature had dropped and the winds had picked up. The bus arrived shortly, but not before Jin got completely soaked. The ride took longer than usual due to several bad car accidents and traffic light outages. At one point, the wind shook the bus so hard, a few people screamed in fear. The wind, the rains, the extremes of the weather were deeply disturbing. Jin feared that he was endangering the people here every time he jumped to Mina's world. The responsibility weighed heavy on his heart. But there was not much he could do about it if he wanted to keep seeing Mina.

Tuesday, April 22

Jin woke up to news of a tornado watch and flooding so severe that parts of Washington, DC, were submerged. He realized that he needed to take a short break from going to Mina's world. There was no doubt in his mind that his activities were causing the severe weather they were dealing with. And it was not just locally. World news was filled with dire warnings of climate change.

Dr. Brennan called him later that day. "I see you stopped by my office," he said. "I'm sorry I missed you. Thank you for the letter. To be honest, I was blown away by it—I didn't know what I was going to say to you."

"I get it," Jin replied. "I don't know what it said, but I can imagine it was still pretty shocking."

"He, that is the other me, told me he married Chandra." Dr. Brennan gave a sad laugh. "I envy him. I still remember being frozen in place as she got off the elevator even as my heart was telling me to go after her. It was the biggest mistake of my life."

"It's not too late," Jin replied. "She never married."

"I see you looked her up," Dr. Brennan said. "Me too. I've also seen her at conferences and events from time to time. Never got up the courage to talk to her again. Maybe I'll reach out to her."

"That would be great. She's really nice. I liked her a lot."

The professor was quiet for a long moment before speaking in a lowered voice. "Jin, I'm going to be off the grid for a while as I deal with some unexpected issues on a project I'm working on. I'll contact you when things quiet down."

"But Professor! I thought you were going to help me . . ."

"It's just a couple of weeks," Dr. Brennan said. "*Please*, don't come to campus. Stay close to home and just wait for my call."

There was an intensity in his low voice that gave Jin pause. He was reminded of the file and his lab reports, which had been set deliberately on the professor's desk. Realization hit Jin. The professor was warning him.

"Okay, Professor," Jin replied. "I'll wait for your call."

"Stay safe," Dr. Brennan said, and hung up the phone.

The call shook Jin deeply. His alarm bells were ringing hard. While he trusted Dr. Brennan completely, he'd been feeling uneasy ever since the professor had mentioned talking to his team. Now Jin knew that something was wrong, and it probably had to do with his lab reports and Dr. Vance. The arrogant doctor had felt off to Jin from the moment he met him. But Jin's gut was now telling him that he had to watch out for Tundra. For some reason, Vance wanted Jin at TULLY and Dr. Brennan did *not*. There was no other reason for him to tell Jin to stay away from campus. Dr. Brennan was trying to protect him.

Easy enough to do, Jin thought. *But does that also mean I shouldn't go see Mina?*

Jin went to his window to look up at the sky. The rain had not let up at all, and there was no sign of the anomaly. He guessed that was a good thing. As much as he wanted to see Mina again, he was morally conflicted by what was happening in his world. In his attempt to save himself, he couldn't endanger the lives of everyone else.

Sunday, April 27

"Jin, we're going to brunch! Wake up! You've got fifteen minutes!"

Groaning, Jin tried to pull the covers over his head.

"No, son, you have to come."

"But you don't even like brunch," Jin complained. His father gave him a sympathetic look as he sat down on the bed next to him.

"Sometimes we've got to take one for the team," he said. "And today your mom is in a 'brunch or else' mood. Last time 'or else' meant cleaning out the garage, remember?"

"I'll get ready," Jin said with a heavy sigh.

"That's my boy!"

In the shower, Jin stood unmoving under the tepid water stream as it slowly began to warm up. He absolutely hated brunch. It felt awkward and uncomfortable for him, as it was almost always in very fancy white spaces where he stood out as the poor little Asian kid adopted by a rich, generous white family. A pang of guilt hit him. He knew that wasn't how

Phil and Alice thought, but still, at brunch it always felt like he was on display.

He let the now hot water calm him. Jin knew the rain had been very hard on Alice. And he also had been difficult to deal with. Going to brunch seemed a small price to pay for his general moodiness.

They got in the car and drove to the Harvest, Alice's favorite brunch restaurant. Jin peered up in the sky and saw no sign of the black hole. The restaurant was in an outdoor mall area with a farmers' market and tons of little stores to shop at. It was crowded with people eager to spend a lovely day outside. At the Harvest, the wait for brunch was over an hour. Phil and Alice headed to the farmers' market. Jin made his way to the bookstore. All the research he had been doing had made him interested in astrophysics. He wanted to see what books might be available at the Book Nook.

Inside the cozy shop, Jin scrolled through the bookshelves but didn't find anything he was looking for. As he wandered the store, he entered a back room with a sitting area. Behind it was a door with a large oval window that showed a brightly lit room. Through the window, Jin could see a lot of people moving about. Curious, he pushed open the door and entered an entirely different bookstore. Shocked, he searched for the doorway he'd entered from and once again saw the quiet, cramped Book Nook space through the oval window. Above the door, a sign read EMPLOYEES ONLY. He immediately realized he was in another world.

The bookstore he was in had several registers behind a large checkout area. A sign that read WORDPLAY hung on the wall above the registers. Jin quickly started his timer, curious to know how long he would stay when, instead of being teleported, he'd walked through what was most likely a portal. He wondered if Mina was nearby. He combed the entire store but didn't find her. Thinking she might be outside, he headed to the front doors but felt a resistance that he couldn't get past. No matter how hard he tried, he couldn't push through it. From behind him, someone loudly said, "Excuse me!" He quickly stepped out of the way in embarrassment. He probably looked weird to the people around him.

Walking over to the large display windows, he peered outside. In front of the store sat a couple on a bench with a large golden retriever and a small white dog that looked like a stuffed animal. He looked up and down the street but didn't see Mina. The block surrounding the store looked very much like the shopping area in his world. He spotted a farmers' market, but the stores across from Wordplay were not the same. Approaching a different exit door, Jin tried to leave again, but to no avail.

Next to the entranceway was a café area with tables filled with people eating, drinking, and reading. He nearly bumped into an older woman with short dark curls and a brown complexion, who looked very familiar to him. She smiled warmly at him and then made her way to a nearby table where two women sat drinking coffee.

"Lucia, I love the new café," one of the women said.

"Yes, and the baked goods are delicious," the other woman agreed.

The short-haired woman thanked them for coming to Wordplay, which made Jin think she might be the owner.

Glancing at his watch, he saw that ten minutes had

passed. But the big difference was that he couldn't leave the area he was in. He was excited to tell Mina and the professors this new development. If this was Mina's world, then they could meet in Wordplay! He was heading toward the back of the store so he could return to the Book Nook when he was stopped by a young bookseller.

"I'm sorry, but this area is for employees only."

Behind her, Jin could see customers browsing the shelves of the Book Nook through the oval window of the EMPLOYEES ONLY doorway.

"Oh, sorry," Jin said. "I was looking for the restroom."

The bookseller pointed to the other side of the store and Jin thanked them. Waiting until all was clear, he snuck out the door and was back in the Book Nook.

Turning around, he gazed in amazement at the portal entrance. Fifteen minutes had now passed, and yet the Wordplay bookstore was still there and accessible. Fascinated, Jin walked outside and looked up at the sky. It was clear and still sunny. There was no anomaly visible. This meant the portal worked even if the black hole in the sky was missing. However, it did not allow him to leave the store area.

He then examined the front of all the shops on the block. Next to the Book Nook was a makeup store, which was much bigger and looked to be about the size of the Wordplay bookstore in Mina's world. He entered the makeup store and walked over to where he thought the portal doorway had been. But here it was just a regular door that had a sign that also read EMPLOYEES ONLY. That had to be the same door that was in Wordplay.

He exited before the salesclerks could ask him what he

wanted and went back into the Book Nook. The portal door was still there.

"This is amazing," Jin said out loud. He wondered what it all meant. It had to be a good sign. Maybe this really was the universe trying to find a way for him to stay in Mina's world. Jin felt excited and hopeful.

Just then his phone beeped and he received a text from his parents.

Mom: Table's ready! Let's eat!

Not wanting to leave empty-handed after walking in and out, Jin picked up a pretty drawing journal for Mina and a box of chocolates in the shape of a book. At the cash register, he did a double take when he saw Lucia, the owner of Wordplay, ringing him up.

"That will be $27.89," she said cheerfully. "Do you have a membership with us?"

Jin shook his head. "Are you the owner?"

Lucia beamed at him. "Yes, I am! It was always my dream to open up my own bookstore," she said. "One day, I hope to have a café attached. But baby steps for now!"

"I think that would be an excellent idea," Jin replied. Smiling at the knowledge that she'd achieved her dream in the other world, he left to join his parents. As he walked down the street, he noticed a large black SUV inching along behind him.

Thinking it was odd, Jin stopped to turn and stare at the driver. The tinted windows were very dark, but he could just make out the outlines of two men. The vehicle continued slowly past him and Jin took note of the license plate.

Having lived in DC all his life, Jin could recognize a government vehicle, and sometimes even unmarked police cars. But this SUV was nondescript. He watched the vehicle intently until it turned out of the area. Shaking off his unease, Jin ran the rest of the way to the restaurant.

CHAPTER 14

Jin's Guilt

Sunday, April 27

Later that same afternoon, Jin noticed that the anomaly had reappeared in the sky, an hour before he was to meet Mina. Knowing this meant he would definitely see her, he showered again and changed several times before choosing a nice button-down and black khakis. He grabbed his backpack with her presents and headed to the park. The weather was perfect. Jin wondered if that meant portals didn't affect the weather, unlike when he teleported. As he sat on the bench and thought of Mina, he felt the buzz that signaled teleporting—which made him realize that he hadn't felt this sensation in the bookstore.

He appeared in Mina's world just as Mina was about to sit down. He reached over to pull her onto his lap.

Mina let out a tiny shriek of surprise before laughing.

"Jin!" She hugged him enthusiastically.

Several moments passed before they pulled apart. Mostly because of the snickering and lewd comments they could hear from nearby teens.

"Come on, let's get out of here," Mina said.

"Where are we going?"

"Away from those obnoxious jerks!"

They ended up walking until they reached Mina's favorite boba shop. After getting their drinks, they sat outside, and Jin passed Mina the bag of gifts he'd bought at the Book Nook.

"I bought you a little something," he said.

"I love it!" Mina exclaimed. She hooked her leg around his and passed Jin her Polaroid camera. "My first gift from my boyfriend! Quick, take a picture for me!"

Mina looked so happy that Jin wished he'd thought to buy her more things.

"With many more to come," he promised.

"I don't need presents, I just need you," she replied before changing the subject. "This must be your local bookstore?" She pointed to the bag with the Book Nook logo.

Jin then told her about what had happened at the bookstore.

"Wordplay! That's my bookstore!" she said. "I didn't go inside, but I was at the bagel shop a few doors down from it. I passed the bookstore on my way home. There were these two dogs in front that I said hello to before I left."

"Wait, a golden retriever and a small white dog?"

"Yes!"

"So it was your world and you were there!" Jin said. "I wonder if that means the portal must still be tied to you in some way."

"But it's weird you couldn't exit the store," she said.

"Even stranger that I didn't get bumped out after a minute."

Mina dug into her fanny pack for her wallet and a small notepad. She pulled out a twenty-dollar bill and gave it to him. "I wish I had more cash, but here, keep this in your wallet to use if you get stuck here," she said. "You can't use your money."

In her notepad, she jotted down her cell phone number. "Try to call or text me next time so I can come meet you."

"But my phone won't work here," he replied.

"More reason to take this money. You may have to ask someone to use their phone."

Jin took the money and the paper she ripped out, folded them together, and placed them in his wallet.

"Good idea," he said. "Why didn't I think of that?"

"Because I'm smarter, clearly," Mina teased.

"I accept that." Jin smiled.

"Will I see you tomorrow also?"

"As long as the black hole is there, I can come," Jin said. "But I think I should wait a few days before I see you again."

"Why?" Mina asked in disappointment.

"Whenever I come back, the weather gets really bad," Jin replied. "It's making me feel guilty about coming." He didn't mention the weakness and exhaustion that he had been feeling. He didn't want to make her feel worse.

"Then when will I see you again?"

"How about Friday?"

Mina frowned. "That feels like a long time."

Jin hugged her tight. "Agreed. Let's make it Thursday. Have you bought your prom dress yet?"

"No, I went shopping with Saachi and Megan yesterday

but we couldn't find anything we liked. We're going to try again later this week and go to Tysons mall. They've got a lot more stores to choose from."

"I'm excited to see what you'll wear! Your homecoming dress was incredible."

"It's going to be hard to beat that," Mina sighed.

"No, it won't, anything you wear will be incredible," Jin said.

By five p.m., Mina was moping.

"Sunday-night dinners are absolute rituals," she sighed. "I have to go now. Dad expects me home by five-thirty."

"You love it," Jin said gently. "It's great bonding time with him."

On their walk home, Mina took Jin on a slightly different route, until they arrived at a town house community different from the ones that Mina and Jin lived in. But right away, he felt a connection. They passed by a small play area that he recognized. Memories of little Mina and himself on the slides and swings bombarded his brain.

"I know this place," Jin said. He almost let go of Mina's hand in excitement, but she linked her arm through his. This time he led the way. Through the narrow streets of the complex, past several rows of quaint town houses until he reached one with a faded blue door.

"This was my house," he said. He could remember the inside clearly. A large living room opening into a dining room and kitchen. It had one more floor upstairs, with two large bedrooms. There was a basement where his mother had her workroom, which opened up to a patio in the back. Their yard would get flooded with so much sunshine that it always filled their house with light.

He felt weak again but also overcome with grief. This was what had been taken away from him. A happy childhood with his mother in this house. His teen years and his cultural roots. Would he even have been the same person he was now if circumstances had been different?

"I wish I could see her," he whispered.

Mina put an arm around his waist and leaned up against him. "You will, Jin. We're going to do everything we can to make that happen."

Her words rang deeply hollow to Jin. As much as he wanted to be a part of her world and see his mother again, there was still no answer to his situation. No solution to what was happening to him.

A sudden dizzy spell hit Jin hard, and he could feel himself nearly blacking out. Not wanting to worry Mina, he smiled weakly.

"You should go now," he said. "I just realized I have to get home soon myself. Let's say goodbye here."

Before she could protest, he kissed her goodbye and gently pushed her away.

Back in his world, his old house looked exactly the same. The faded blue door opened suddenly and an old woman stepped out and stared suspiciously at him.

"Can I help you?" she asked in a sharp tone.

"Sorry," he responded hoarsely. "I'm in the wrong place."

Jin slowly headed home. He was no longer weak physically, but he felt emotionally drained.

* * *

Like clockwork, the bad weather started as soon as Jin got home. During dinner, Phil had the news playing in the background, something he had started doing ever since the weather became so unstable. They all turned toward the television in the living room when breaking news announced a massive twenty-car accident on the beltway. The screen showed tall plumes of black smoke billowing from an overturned tractor trailer. Fire trucks, ambulances, and police cars were all at the scene.

"Oh no, that's terrible," Alice breathed.

Phil shook his head. "It's dangerous out there."

Jin's heart thudded painfully as they heard the announcer report on multiple casualties. His guilt clawed at his stomach. Had he not gone to see Mina, would those people be alive today? He needed to talk with Dr. Brennan. Losing his appetite, Jin excused himself from the table and went to his room to call the professor, but his call went right to voicemail. Trembling with guilt, Jin decided he wouldn't go to Mina's world until he could meet with the professor.

CHAPTER 15

Being Followed

Friday, May 2

On college T-shirt day Jin forgot to wear the Johns Hopkins shirt that his parents had purchased for him.

"Hey, have you noticed that a lot of schools have red shirts?" Liam asked. He was wearing a blue shirt with UCSD in yellow letters.

"You're right! Red must be a popular school color," Sam remarked. He flaunted a bright orange Syracuse T-shirt.

"That's because half the seniors are going to UMD and their school color is red." Mark rolled his eyes.

"Oh, I see," Liam said. "That explains it."

"Y'all are just not very observant," Mark stated.

"I blame all the rain," Liam responded. "It's giving me brain rot."

"Yeah, I'm sick of being inside all the time," Sam said. "Let's go to the rec center later."

When school ended, Jin went with his friends to play ball. Out of a deep sense of guilt, he'd missed his meeting with Mina yesterday, and he'd still had no luck reaching Dr. Brennan. He'd called and texted but there'd been no response at all. He hoped nothing bad had happened to the professor, but he couldn't shake the fear that something was terribly wrong. The file with Vance's notes kept haunting his mind.

Bring subject to TULLY immediately.

Jin wasn't supposed to have read this—but Dr. Brennan had left the confidential papers exposed so that Jin couldn't miss them. And now he couldn't reach the professor. *He's probably really busy and ignoring my calls. There's nothing to worry about. He said he needed some time.*

Jin tried to shake off his concerns. Maybe hanging with his friends would help keep his mind from overloading. They all piled into Mark's car. In the rearview mirror, Jin noticed a large black SUV following them. He turned to look more closely, but Liam and Sam were acting goofy and blocking his view. When they pulled into the parking lot of the rec center, the black SUV slowly continued past.

Mark shook Jin's shoulder, making him flinch.

"Whoa! Why are you so jumpy?"

"I thought that black SUV was following us 'cause you ran that stop sign."

He pointed to the SUV at the traffic light.

They all turned to look.

"There's no way it's an unmarked police car," Liam said. "Those are all Ford Explorers or Chevy Tahoes. That's a Lincoln Navigator. Too pricey to be a cop car."

But not for Tundra Labs. Jin thought back to the vehicle he'd seen before. It looked like the same car, but he wasn't certain.

"I think I saw that car before," he said.

His friends all laughed.

"Jin, this is Washington, DC, all you see are black SUVs everywhere," Liam said.

"My dad drives a black Explorer and my mom drives a Suburban," Mark said.

"Why does your mom drive the bigger car?" Sam asked.

" 'Cause she's the better driver," Mark replied.

"Our moms drive minivans and it's nothing to be ashamed of, right, Sam?" Liam asked as he slung an arm around Sam's shoulders.

"I hate it," Sam replied shortly. "Driving a minivan on a date is the worst."

"Liam wouldn't know," Mark chimed in.

"Hey! It's not that bad," Liam argued as the friends all walked into the rec center.

Jin took one last look at the vehicle. He could've sworn the men in the car were both staring at him.

On the court, Jin played poorly, missing every shot. He tripped over his own feet. To the frustration of his friends, he couldn't even pass the ball. He began compensating for his poor play by aggressively fouling and running down every loose ball. A larger player named Stan, who was known for constant smack talking, began to target Jin.

"Yo, get this K-pop boy out of my face before I put him down!"

Mark and Liam pulled Jin aside before things got worse.

"Take it easy," Mark cautioned. "This is supposed to be a friendly game. We don't want to fight anyone."

But Jin couldn't control himself, as if this was the only way to let out all his frustrations. After a wild tussle for a rebound, Jin was violently elbowed in the eye hard enough for it to start bleeding. Jin tried to insist that he could keep playing, but Mark and Liam dragged him off the basketball court, holding a towel to his head.

"What's up, bro?" Mark asked. "You're off your game today."

"I know, sorry about that," Jin replied. He told himself that he was imagining things, but the tension still sat in the pit of his stomach. Taking a deep breath, he tried to focus solely on the moment.

It didn't help—Jin was still distracted. In his mind's eye, he kept seeing the SUV driving slowly past him at the shopping center and the parking lot. By the time the game was over, he was still angry and frustrated.

"Hey, let's go to the diner for a bite to eat and then hang out at my place," Mark said. "It'll be good for you."

"We need to shower first, because y'all stink," Sam said.

"No, that was just Jin," Liam said.

"Jin, you need to take that stick out of your ass and come to the diner in an hour."

"So that's why you sucked so bad," Liam joked.

"At least I can take the stick out, what's your excuse?" Jin snapped.

Sam and Mark burst out laughing.

"Jin, you made a joke! Good one, man," Liam snarked.

Mark drove everyone home. As Jin got out of the car, Mark yelled, "One hour, or I'm coming back to get you."

Jin waved his friend off and entered his house. He was surprised to find his parents in the foyer all dressed up.

"Hey hon, you're on your own tonight," Alice said. "We've got tickets to the Kennedy Center, and we have to leave now so that we can get dinner and still make it to the show on time. You know how slow your father eats."

"I am vilified just because I like to taste my food!" Phil complained.

Alice pushed him out the door.

"We'll be late!" Alice and Phil waved goodbye and left.

Relieved to have the house to himself, Jin ran all the way upstairs to his room and took a long hot shower. He could feel some of his tension melt away. Perhaps dinner with his friends would be good for him. Something to take his mind off all his troubles. He had finished dressing when he heard the beep of the front door alarm and the door opening and shutting. Thinking it was Phil and Alice coming back, he ran downstairs.

"Did you guys forget your tickets or something?" he asked as he entered the main-floor living area—then came to an abrupt stop. Dr. Vance, the man who had taken his blood tests, was sitting at his dining room table.

"How'd *you* get in here?" Jin asked in complete shock.

"I rang the doorbell and no one answered. After a few minutes I realized the door was open," Dr. Vance said. "Which seemed unsafe to me. I came in to see if you were all right."

He's lying, Jin thought. *No way was the door unlocked. I heard it slam. But how the hell did he get our alarm code?*

Jin was angry but cautious. This man looked too comfortable for someone who had broken into another person's house.

"I'm about to go meet my friends for dinner," Jin said. "Where's Dr. Brennan? Why are you here?"

Dr. Vance leaned forward and clasped his hands together. "Jin, Dr. Brennan had to go out of town on a personal emergency. But he told me everything about you and your exploits, and we at Tundra Labs believe we can help you."

All of Jin's senses were heightened in alarm. This whole situation felt dangerous.

Plastering on a fake conciliatory smile, Jin said, "Okay, that's great! Can we talk about this another time? I'm late to dinner."

"I'd like to have you come down to TULLY, where you'll be able to see exactly what we can do for you," Dr. Vance said. "You've heard about TULLY, right? It's the most advanced laboratory in the world. It's only about a two-hour drive. Fascinating place, if I say so myself. You'll love it. I'll have my staff drive you down. When are you available?"

Jin's stomach cramped with anxiety. Dr. Vance had broken into his house in his determination to get Jin to a deep-underground prison. His gut was telling him he was not safe with this man.

Keeping his expression neutral, Jin shook his head. "Oh, that's way too far, my parents won't agree to me going all the way over there. I was thinking on campus or in your DC office or something."

The other man paused, staring at Jin for a long moment.

"We can really only help you from TULLY," Dr. Vance said with a frown. "I'd like to have a conversation with your parents. They can come also if they want."

"That would be really awkward because I haven't told them anything," Jin said.

"I'm sure we can come up with a plausible reason," Dr. Vance said with a fake smile. "After all, you are entering Johns Hopkins as a pre-med student. And we have renowned university professors who work closely with us on a variety of research programs. I'm sure your father, as an alum, would be very aware of our research programs with both the undergrad and medical schools."

Suppressing a shudder, Jin shook his head. Dr. Vance knew too much about him and his family.

"I would prefer to speak with Dr. Brennan first. They only know about him."

Dr. Vance continued to gaze at Jin with cold disapproval. The silence enveloped the room. Just as Jin wondered what else he could possibly say, the other man rose to his feet abruptly.

"I understand," Dr. Vance said. From a pocket inside his jacket, he pulled out a small, slim case. He opened it and showed a thumb drive in the box. "In the meantime, Dr. Brennan asked me to give this to you. Please keep this case with you at all times so that when you go to the other universe you can give it to the other Dr. Brennan. The case will keep the data from getting corrupted during transport."

Jin knew that there was no reason he needed a case for a thumb drive. Tundra Labs was going to use this to monitor him.

Jin reluctantly took the case. He didn't want to make Dr. Vance suspicious by refusing it.

"I'll put it in my backpack, since I always carry that when I teleport."

"And when do you think that will be?" Dr. Vance asked with keen interest.

“I try every day,” Jin replied. “But I can’t control it.”

Dr. Vance nodded. “Well, just let me know when it happens.” He took out his business card and placed it and the thumb drive case on the table.

“I will.”

After Dr. Vance left, Jin examined the case carefully. It probably had some sort of tracking device or a recorder, not that Jin could see it. The likelihood of it working in the other world was zero, which meant Dr. Vance, or Tundra Labs, was using it solely to track where Jin was and when he teleported. Jin just didn’t understand why they wanted to keep tabs on him.

He opened the case and took out the thumb drive. He was curious to see what was on it. But when he plugged it into his computer, it immediately asked for a George University password.

Staring at the case made Jin furious. Vance had been watching his house and had brazenly broken in, knowing that he was alone. The black SUV had probably been following him for a while. Vance was pressuring Jin to go to TULLY, and the only person who could help was missing. Jin tamped down his rising fear. He reminded himself that he wasn’t all alone. He had Mina, Dr. Prescott, and the other Dr. Brennan. They were trying to help him. But they weren’t here in this world.

It was clear that Vance was not someone who was used to being refused. Jin knew he’d have to be very careful teleporting from now on.

CHAPTER 16

Dr. Brennan Is Missing!

Saturday, May 3

In the morning, the sun shone bright in the clear blue sky. No clouds or black holes in sight. Jin woke to his phone blowing up with texts.

Mark: hoops?

Liam: absolutely

Sam: when

Mark: anytime after 2

Liam: im down

Sam: ok but i might cut out early

Liam: ?

Sam: got ap physics on mon calc 1 on thurs

Mark: shut up ive got 7

Sam: why would you do that

Liam: u know more dont make u smarter

Mark: my mom made me

Liam: this why im glad my mom dont speak english

Sam: you barely speak it

Liam: ur mom

Sam: 😂

Mark: jin you coming

Jin: yes

On his way out, Jin noticed a black SUV parked on his street. There were two men wearing sunglasses, just sitting in the vehicle. They weren't even trying to be inconspicuous.

As he biked past their vehicle, he could see their heads

turning to watch him, but they didn't move. Relieved, Jin rode quickly to the park.

But the fact that they didn't follow him didn't mean they weren't watching him. After last night's encounter with Dr. Vance, Jin was confident he was being followed. Vance definitely wanted to know when Jin was teleporting.

At the park, his friends were waiting for him.

"Jin, you're still coming to prom with us, right?" Mark asked.

"Uh, yeah," he replied. Prom reminded Jin of Mina and their promise to try to be there together.

"We've rented a party bus to take us to DC for pics, dinner, and then prom," Mark said. "Since we got about twenty-five people, the bus will cost us like fifty each. Cool?"

"Yeah, that sounds good," Liam said.

Jin nodded and wondered what Mina would be doing. He wished he could rent a limo to pick up Mina and escort her to prom himself. To be honest, it was madness to even think they could go to prom together, but Jin was hopeful that the universe would allow them this chance.

As they played, Jin saw a black SUV parked directly across from the basketball court. They *were* following him.

Jin continued trying to reach Dr. Brennan, with no luck. He even called the physics department and discovered that Dr. Brennan's classes had been taken over by his teaching assistants while he dealt with a personal matter.

A sick foreboding sat in the pit of his stomach. What if something bad had happened to the professor? Was this also his fault? For over a week, he'd been avoiding meeting

Mina. The good news was that the weather had been beautiful, and it had also calmed down across the globe. Jin had kept himself as busy as possible, trying not to think of Mina, especially when the anomaly appeared above him. He avoided any emotional thoughts about the situation, and it had worked. He had not teleported anywhere. But his heart hurt and it was becoming harder and harder to hide his feelings.

At home, Jin holed up in his room and tried to call Dr. Brennan again. This time he received a text from Dr. Brennan's number.

Dr. Brennan: Jin. I'm sorry I couldn't talk to you before I left. I had to fly out to California for a family emergency.

I'm afraid I'm going to be here for a while. I've briefed Dr. Vance fully on your situation and he will be able to help you.

As Jin read the text message, a chill ran down his spine. He remembered when Dr. Brennan had said, *You can text me, but my apologies if I never respond. My fingers are too clumsy for the tiny buttons. You can always email me.*

This text was *not* from Dr. Brennan.

Looking at the business card Dr. Vance had given him at their last meeting, he realized it was different from the first one he'd received. Rummaging through his desk drawer, he found the previous business card. It read:

DR. MARTIN VANCE
DIRECTOR OF DIAGNOSTIC RADIOLOGY
AND NUCLEAR MEDICINE
TUNDRA LABS

The new card read:

DR. MARTIN VANCE
GLOBAL DEVELOPMENT DIRECTOR
TUNDRA LABS

Why did the man have two different business cards? Jin did a quick Google search, which brought up a recent article that announced a $4.5 billion contract with Tundra Labs from the Department of Defense for research and development on the study of black holes, space science and engineering, information technology, simulation modeling, operations analysis, and combat systems.

Dr. Vance, global development director, was the head of the program that had received the grant from the DOD. Alarm bells were going off in Jin's head. The first business card was a lie. Vance had never been director of diagnostic radiology and nuclear medicine. Jin could only assume he'd been lied to so that he'd agree to take the blood tests. But had Dr. Brennan been in on the deception? That really troubled him. However, he couldn't worry about that. What if something had happened to Dr. Brennan and someone was impersonating him to convince Jin to trust Dr. Vance? The black SUVs were definitely following him, and he needed to talk to someone. The only person he could now trust was the Dr. Brennan in Mina's world. But the weather had been stable lately. He didn't want to send his world into danger again.

He felt like he was on an emotional roller coaster headed toward a nervous breakdown. It pained him that his guilt and fear overpowered his desire to see Mina. He stared at the Polaroid of Mina that he'd propped on his desk. Mina had given him a lot of pictures, but this was his favorite. It was the one of her holding the gifts he'd bought her from the Book Nook. She'd been so happy about a journal and a small box of chocolates.

"The bookstore!"

He wondered if the portal in Book Nook was still there. If it was, he could call Mina to meet him there. When he'd used it the first time, there'd been no adverse weather. Maybe the portal was a way to avoid harming his world. But he had to do it without alerting the men following him.

Sunday, May 4

"Damn it! Why can't they give it a rest?"

Jin stared out his bedroom window at the black SUV that had been there all morning. The men weren't even bothering to hide the fact that they had him under surveillance. Their stony faces and intimidating air gave off military vibes. It made Jin not want to leave his house for fear of running into them alone. Not that he thought they would hurt him. But he didn't like being monitored.

He debated telling his father, but how would he explain what was happening? He didn't even want to tell Ms. A about how Dr. Brennan might have gone missing for fear of something happening to her also.

As he stared down at the men, he saw a neighbor from

across the street go up to the car and begin to yell at the driver. He recognized her as the woman who would always get into fights with people about street parking. Just then he got an idea.

Grabbing his phone, he called 911.

"Hi, I'd like to report a black SUV with these two creepy guys that keep harassing women in my neighborhood."

After giving the address of the house the vehicle was parked in front of, Jin grinned as he hung up the phone and sat at his window and waited. Less than ten minutes had passed when a patrol car pulled up. The officers spoke with the men for several minutes before the SUV took off.

They were probably lurking nearby, but Jin felt relieved not to have them right in front of his house. However, he needed a plan if he was going to get to the bookstore without being followed.

Jin knew the thumb drive case was the way Dr. Vance and Tundra were tracking or spying on him. But if he left it at home, they would know. He just needed to convince them that he was trying to teleport and not let them know when he actually did.

Opening his bag, Jin took out the case, removed the drive, and stuck it in his pocket. He then stuffed the case into a thick sock and taped it over with bubble wrap. If it was a recording device, he hoped it would be too muffled to hear anything. He also threw a black cap and white T-shirt into the bag.

Next, he texted Sam and asked him if he could stop by. Of his friends, Sam lived the closest to the bookstore. Once he received an affirmative response, he left the house and walked around the neighborhood. He spotted the black SUV right away. Glancing at his watch, Jin saw that it was one p.m. He went to the park and sat at a picnic table, pretending to study for his AP Psychology test. From the corner of his eye, he caught sight of the black SUV pulling into the parking lot. When thirty minutes had passed, he packed up his bag and walked the seven blocks to the bus stop. He could see the SUV following behind. Once on the bus, he watched as the car drove past. He realized that if there really was a tracker in the case Dr. Vance gave him, then they didn't have to physically follow him. Deciding to test it out, Jin got off the bus a stop early and quickly cut down a dead-end street. There he climbed over the fence into the alleyways, where he slipped in and out until he was sure he would have lost anyone following him. He was only a few blocks from Sam's building when he saw the SUV turning the corner.

"Tracking confirmed," Jin muttered to himself.

As he was buzzing Sam's apartment, Jin caught sight of the SUV parking on the street in front of the building.

"Yo, Jin, what's up?" Sam asked as he let him into his apartment.

"Sorry to bother your family today," Jin said.

"Nah, it's cool, my folks are both working at the restaurant and I gotta stay home and babysit my brother Joey," Sam said.

"You're not babysitting me! I'm twelve!" a voice yelled from the other room.

Sam snickered. He walked toward his room but banged on the closed door next to it first, shouting, "You're not twelve yet, dork."

"Poophead!" Joey yelled.

Sam smiled and went into his room.

"I thought you had to study?" he asked Jin as he sprawled on his bed.

"Yeah, I do," Jin replied as he took in Sam's room. "But I've gotta go and meet someone now and I don't want to bring my bag. Mind if I leave it in your room and come get it later tonight?"

"No problem, just leave it anywhere," Sam said. He was already engrossed in his gaming console.

Jin took the cap and white T-shirt out of his bag and quickly changed out of his black shirt. Seeing a large closet, he opened it to find a huge mess. There was more clothing strewn all over the floor than on hangers. He shoved his bag into the deepest corner and covered it with a heap of clothes.

"What the hell are you doing?" Sam asked, sitting up and peering at Jin strangely. "You got something in there you shouldn't?"

"Ha! Hell no," Jin replied. "I don't want it in the way. So I'm hiding it."

Sam blinked at him. "You realize you're acting weird, right?"

"Yeah, I know."

Clapping his hands together, Jin grinned awkwardly.

"Er, thanks, Sam," Jin said. He'd started to the door when he remembered about the SUV parked in front of the building. "Hey, if I go the back way does it shortcut to Spring Valley?"

"Yeah, but you gotta go down to G One and exit through the side door next to the garage entrance," Sam said.

"Okay, thanks. You want anything? I'll be back by sixish and I can bring you something from Bread & Butter."

This made Sam put his console down. "Hell yeah! Can you get me one of the ham-and-cheese sandwiches and kettle chips?"

"Me too!" Joey shouted from his room. This time his door opened and a miniature version of Sam stepped out. "Hi, Jin, can you get me a roast beef and cheese and a grape Fanta?"

"Hey!" Sam threw a pillow at Joey. "He didn't ask you if you wanted anything."

"It's okay, Jin likes me." Joey grinned as he dodged the pillow, and then whispered, "I don't get why you're friends with him. He's a wet toilet seat."

"I heard that, creep."

"I got you covered." Jin winked at Joey. "But one of you is gonna have to open the garage door when I come back so I don't have to walk all the way around the block."

"Joey will do it," Sam said immediately.

Joey looked resigned but nodded. "Only for you, Jin, not for Stank Butt."

"That's a dead little man talking right there," Sam drawled.

Before they could escalate the fight, Jin left Sam's place and took the elevator down to level G1. The garage was huge and dimly lit. Jin was wondering which way to go when a large vehicle suddenly appeared, driving toward him. Jin froze. His heart pounded rapidly in his chest as he thought the Tundra men had found him. But it was a dark blue SUV that parked next to the elevators, and a large family poured out of the doors, dropping bags, toys, and snacks all over the ground. Avoiding the now screaming children, Jin walked in the direction the car had come from, hunting for the exit. When he finally found it, he rushed through the side door next to the garage entrance. The back of the building opened onto another street. Jin pulled his cap down low and anxiously looked around before taking off at a run. By the time he got to the shopping center, it was a quarter after three.

He ran for the Book Nook and walked in right behind a group of women. Once inside, he made a beeline to the back door, anxious to see if the portal was working. His heart had been beating erratically since leaving Sam's. It calmed as soon as he saw another bookstore showing through the door's window. With a deep sigh of relief, he went through the portal and entered Wordplay.

The brightly lit store was busy and had music playing. It couldn't be more different from the small, cramped bookstore he had just been in. His mood immediately lifted.

Spotting an information desk, Jin walked over and asked if he could use the telephone. He pulled out the paper Mina had given him and called her number, relieved when she answered it right away.

"Hello?" Mina asked in a curious voice.

"Mina! It's Jin. I'm at the bookstore, can you come meet me? I need to talk with the professors. It's urgent."

Jin had not been waiting long when Mina came charging toward him, her face lit up with a huge smile. Jin realized he could never get tired of seeing her so happy to see him. He loved her too much.

"You're here!" Mina exclaimed. "Does that mean while we're in the store, I don't have to constantly be touching you?"

"Yeah, something about being in here is different," Jin replied.

"What if I want to hold your hand anyway?" Mina teased.

“Anytime, I’m all yours.”

Mina’s laugh was joyful and filled Jin’s heart. He knew that all he wanted from life was to be in the same world with her, no matter what it took.

“I wish we could stay here all day, but I really need to talk to Dr. Prescott and Dr. Brennan as soon as possible,” Jin said.

Without any hesitation, Mina called the professors, and they were soon on their way to meet them.

Twenty minutes later, Dr. Prescott ushered them into a very sleek and modern apartment. The living room was filled with expensive contemporary furniture, beautiful paintings, and other art pieces that Mina admired. The shelves were also filled with photos of their various trips around the world. The only thing out of place was the huge leather reclining chair positioned next to a minimalist white contemporary sofa.

“When Al and I realized we couldn’t have children, we decided to collect art and experiences instead,” Dr. Prescott said. “There was a time when we were sad about it, but now we live our life to the fullest.”

Dr. Brennan brought over several glasses of iced tea and a plate of fruit, cheeses, and crackers and sat in the reclining chair. “Tell me what’s going on, Jin.”

“I think something bad has happened to my Dr. Brennan,” Jin said. “He’s gone missing.”

CHAPTER 17

The Danger of Tundra Labs

Sunday, May 4

Everyone froze in shock at his words. Jin could feel Mina's hands clutching at his arm painfully.

"He told me there was a problem he had to take care of, but he sounded nervous. And he left my lab reports on his desk. And then that Tundra guy who took my blood showed up inside my house, like broke into my house! He kept insisting that he was helping Dr. Brennan and that I had to go with him to TULLY, but I refused and then he gave me this thumb drive to bring back to you, but it was in a case that was definitely bugged. And he was having me followed. And I got a text from Dr. Brennan saying he was in California. But it was a text and he told me he never texts and I don't think it was him. It had to be someone pretending to be him. And I'm scared."

"Calm down, Jin," Dr. Brennan said. "Let's take it from the beginning again. Slowly."

Jin took deep breaths as he tried to rein in his emotions. Speaking of all that had happened to him for the first time had put into words the fear and stress he'd been under. Explaining it all to the two professors and Mina felt cathartic.

When he was done, Dr. Brennan's lips tightened into a flat line and he exchanged a serious look with his wife. "I'm going to check this thumb drive now," he said. "Chandra, you go ahead and share your findings with them."

Dr. Prescott gazed after her husband with concerned eyes before turning back to Jin and Mina.

"What is it?" Jin asked.

"Let's wait until Al sees what's on the drive," she responded. "In the meantime, I think I have a plausible theory on what the anomaly in the sky is. Physicists from UC Santa Cruz built a simulated multiverse. They wanted to see what would happen when two bubble universes collided. And this is what they came up with."

Jin and Mina peered at the picture on the computer monitor: what looked like an elongated oval split in half with scattered colored dots on one side, and a disk of concentric circles with a completely black center on the other. Dr. Prescott pointed to the disk.

"They found that when bubble universes collide it caused a massive temperature flare in the cosmic microwave background, which would show up in the sky as a disk. Like your anomaly."

"You think the thing in the sky is because the two worlds are colliding?" Jin asked. "Then why isn't it always there?"

"I did some modeling of my own, and I believe that the disk is always present but very faint," Dr. Prescott said, pulling up another computer simulation. "But the severe weather instability you mentioned may be why it's more visible at some times than others."

"But if it's always there, then why can I only teleport when it's actually visible? That doesn't make sense," Jin said.

"Or maybe it does," Dr. Prescott mused. "Perhaps whatever energy is pulling you to this world is strong enough only when it's visible. But what we don't know is how and why. It's all a mystery."

That reminded Jin of the photos the other Dr. Brennan had developed. "Here are the photos of the black hole," he said. "It does kind of look like that disk thing."

Dr. Prescott examined the photos closely, particularly the first one, which showed the blue sky framing the black hole.

"It is really hard to make out what exactly it is," she said. "But it's definitely not a black hole as we know it. I think it seems most similar in shape to my simulation disk."

At that moment, Dr. Brennan returned with a laptop and sat down across from Jin with a serious expression.

"The drive had nothing of relevance on it," Dr. Brennan said. "It was nothing more than a trigger beacon to alert them to the fact that you came here."

"It was a trick?" Jin asked.

"I fear that you may be in danger, Jin," Dr. Brennan continued. "Tundra Labs here is one of those private institutions that has been cited for research misconduct and falsifying data. They are dirty. Do you know the name of the man who came to your house?"

"Dr. Martin Vance, director of something something," Jin said.

Husband and wife glanced at each other in concern.

"He's CEO in this universe," Dr. Brennan replied, showing

them the screen of his laptop. "He's a multibillionaire and a narcissistic sociopath. He has done more harm to this country than any other individual in recent history."

Jin immediately saw Dr. Vance's photo with his title, CEO of Tundra Labs.

"Yeah, I knew I didn't like him. But CEO? That's a big jump from director, right?" Jin asked.

"Huge. Four years ago, he was instrumental in landing a four-point-five-billion-dollar contract from the Department of Defense," Dr. Prescott continued. "With that money, he created a new kind of rocket and launched the biggest satellite communications network, Stormlink, which increased the valuation of Tundra by twelve billion. He was made CEO a month ago."

"He got that contract last year, in my world," Jin remarked. "That means he's three years behind?"

"It took him fifteen months to successfully launch the satellites," Dr. Prescott said. "He's probably in the midst of coordinating the rocket launches. But think about what would cause him to have a major setback."

Jin blinked. "The weather."

The professor nodded. "Severe weather conditions must be hampering his project."

"So when my Dr. Brennan talked about my jumps affecting the weather . . ."

"It was important enough for Vance to get involved. And I think I know why he wants you at TULLY so badly."

"Why?"

"The Tundra Labs in your world is also privately owned. And just like the version here, it has a large underground laboratory built in an old gold mine in Virginia," Dr. Brennan said. "It is one of the few labs in the world where you can study dark matter shielded from the sun and space."

Dr. Prescott gasped. "That would be monstrous! You can't believe he would do that?"

Jin was confused. "Do what?"

"Think about it—if you need the unknown anomaly that appears in your sky to teleport, what would happen if there was four thousand feet of rock between you and it?" Dr. Brennan asked.

"I'd stay in my world?"

"Correct. Because keeping you in your world could theoretically stop it from merging back with the original one, but you would literally be imprisoned underground for the rest of your life," Dr. Brennan said.

"That's evil!" Mina was aghast.

"Would he really imprison me?" Jin asked. "He can't be that bad, can he?"

"It's kidnapping and false imprisonment. And then if he were to subject him to illegal experimentation? It could kill him. Do you really think he'd go that far?"

"Yes. I believe he would. The Dr. Vance of this world is ambitious and unethical and wouldn't hesitate to do so," Dr. Brennan said. "Tundra Labs have men on staff who have done far worse."

"What do you mean far worse? You mean they would kill Jin?" Mina asked.

"The scientists at Tundra Lab would rather have Jin alive so that they can study him," Dr. Brennan said. "But if Jin is dead, it solves Dr. Vance's problem also."

"Jin, you can't go back!" Mina said in a panic, throwing her arms around him as if to physically keep him in place.

Hugging her tight, Jin breathed deeply. He thought of the men in the black SUV that were tracking him. He'd never gotten a good look at their faces.

"Mina, you can't hold on to me forever, and we have to come up with some kind of solution."

He faced the professors again, needing to ask the question he was dreading to ask.

"What about the other Dr. Brennan?" he asked. "Is he really in California on family business?"

The professors were silent, and then Dr. Brennan said, "Jin, I don't have any family in California."

Jin dropped his head in his hands. "Is he dead?" he whispered.

"Or imprisoned in TULLY," Dr. Brennan replied. "I like to believe that they're keeping him alive because they need him once they catch you also. In either case, I'm relieved to know that the other me tried to help you."

"The other you is a very good man," Jin said, his voice hoarse with emotion.

Rising to his feet, he stumbled as he almost blacked out.

"What's the matter?" Dr. Prescott asked in alarm. "You've gotten very pale."

"This has happened before, Jin, from overstaying your time here, correct?"

Looking at their concerned faces, Jin admitted to feeling weak. "Yeah, the longer I stay here, the weaker I am, like all my energy is being drained," he said.

"As if you're disappearing?" Dr. Prescott asked gently.

Jin's eyes widened in shock. That was exactly how he felt.

"Why do you say that?" he asked.

She pointed to where Mina gripped Jin's arm. "Unlike

Mina, who said she was able to enter your world and traverse it, you are physically being kept here," she said. "The longer you stay, the stronger the universe will pull to put you back in your own world. Eventually your physical form here will disappear."

Mina gasped in shock and pulled away from Jin, but he held on to her.

"What happens to me?"

"In theory, you should just reappear in your own world," she said. "In reality, we don't know."

Before Mina could freak out, Dr. Prescott put up her hand. "But I think this may be a good sign."

"It is?" Jin asked.

"If your world is merging back into this one, there must be a way to anchor you in place. We know the key is Mina. She's the one who keeps pulling you here. We just have to figure out how to make it permanent."

"How?" Mina demanded.

"We don't know yet."

"That's just great! How are we supposed to keep Jin safe when he's home?" Mina asked.

Mina looked both frustrated and scared. Just the way Jin felt deep in his core. He took her hand and squeezed it.

"It's okay, Mina, they can't take me to TULLY against my will," he reassured her. "I won't let them."

"Jin, you need to build a case against Vance and Tundra Labs," Dr. Brennan said. "File a police report."

"The police will never believe me!"

"You said an SUV is following you. Record them, collect evidence that they're stalking you. Believe me, they don't want negative attention. And whatever you do, don't be alone with Dr. Vance."

Jin didn't want to say that the advice was not helpful, so he just nodded. "Thanks for your help. Mina and I should go now."

"Jin, we will do everything we can to find a solution for you," Dr. Prescott said. "We're not going to give up on you."

CHAPTER 18

Attack of the Angry Best Friends

Sunday, May 4

The two friends walked slowly back to the bus stop. Jin could feel Mina's anxious gaze on him the entire time, but he didn't know what to say. On the bus, he put his arm around her and pulled her close. "It's okay, I promise I'll be fine," he said. "I'll just go back to my world before there's any chance of me disappearing."

Mina had a death grip on his hand.

"It's okay, Mina," he said. "I'm going to be fine."

"As soon as you get back, tell your parents and Ms. A about what's happening to you. Tell your friends and teachers. The more people are aware of what the Tundra Labs guy is planning, the safer you'll be."

"I don't know how I'm supposed to explain this to my parents," Jin sighed.

"But tell Ms. A at least!"

"I don't think it will make a difference," Jin said.

"Tell her anyway!"

Jin was looking out the window and realized they were near Wordplay. Pulling Mina onto her feet, he pressed the button for the next stop.

"Where are we going?" she asked.

"Come with me. There's something I want to check out," he said.

Getting off the bus, they walked over to Spring Valley shopping center. It was six p.m. and the area was crowded with people on the sidewalks and in the restaurants.

They were right in front of Wordplay when Mina was almost pulled away from him by two girls who stared at him with intense curiosity.

"OH MY GOD! Mina Lee, how dare you!" A tall, beautiful South Asian girl glared murder at Mina.

"That's definitely the guy from her webcomic, right, Saachi?" said a white girl with curly light brown hair who was less angry and far more curious. "He looks just like him!"

"Yes, Megan, and someone is going to die tonight," Saachi fumed.

Mina let out an anxious squeak and hid behind Jin, clutching him from behind. "Guys, I've wanted to tell you everything, but you wouldn't have believed me. I'm so sorry."

"Start talking now and it just might save your life," Saachi said.

"What are you doing? Run for *my* life!" Mina yell-whispered to Jin.

"But first, hello, my name is Megan, and this is Saachi, we are Mina's ex–best friends, and you are?" Megan asked.

Jin smiled at them. "I'm Jin, I'm a really old friend of Mina's."

"Oh, an old friend? Really? I wonder why we've never heard of you or seen you before?" Saachi's eyes were shooting laser beams of anger at him.

"It's very nice to meet you, now it's time to die, Mina," Saachi announced.

Mina whimpered as she wrapped her arms around Jin's back and spun him between herself and her determined friends, who kept trying to pull her away.

"Come here, Mina."

"You can't hide behind him forever."

"Yes, I can."

"We just want to talk to you privately."

"I am a penguin adrift in a sea of killer whales," Mina stated.

Finding himself being flung back and forth between Mina and her friends, Jin put up his hands and said, "I know it's hard to believe, but if she lets go of me, I'll disappear."

This caught their attention right away.

"Huh?"

"Bad idea!" Mina whispered.

"What are you saying? If Mina lets go of you, you plan on running out on her?" This time the nice friend, Megan, looked ready to kill him.

"That's not what he meant—" Mina tried to say.

"You be quiet." Saachi pointed at Mina.

"You keep talking," Saachi said as she crossed her arms and glared at Jin.

Feeling the exhaustion threatening to overcome him, Jin noticed several open tables through the bookstore window. He pointed and said, "Let's sit there and talk."

Once inside, Jin began to feel better. He made his way toward the café, pulling Mina along, her friends following so closely he could feel their angry breaths on his skin.

Mina sat next to Jin, her arm linked through his, and her two friends sat opposite them, both with fierce expressions.

"What's going on?" Megan asked.

"And don't try to lie to us, Mina, we've known something has been wrong with you for months," Saachi said.

Mina looked at Jin.

"They're your best friends, they'll believe you," he said.

Mina took a deep breath. "It all started with the webcomic," she began. Thirty minutes later, Jin and Mina stared back at the baffled expressions on Saachi's and Megan's faces. Then the questions started.

"That is the craziest story I ever heard," Saachi remarked.

"And yet I believe it," Megan replied. "Does that make me the weirdo?"

"We're the weirdos," Saachi agreed.

For the next thirty minutes, Jin and Mina were bombarded with every sort of question. Saachi grilled Jin about his family and grades and schooling, while Megan wanted to know all the differences between their worlds. But mostly, they wanted to see what happened when Mina let go of Jin.

Mina immediately let go of Jin's arm, but nothing happened.

Saachi and Megan glared at him. "You're still here."

"It's because this store is a portal," Jin said with a grin. "If she'd let go of me outside, I would have disappeared, but it works differently here. Let me show you."

Jin walked to the portal between the two bookstores. He could see the Book Nook on the other side of the EMPLOYEES ONLY door.

"This door takes me to my world, into a bookstore called the Book Nook."

Mina and her friends peered through the window, clearly confused.

"All we can see is a supply room," Saachi said.

"Trust me, it's there," Jin said.

Hugging Mina, he asked, "Can you meet on Tuesday at twelve?"

Seeing her nod, he opened the door and stepped to the other side. He turned around and saw Mina and her friends peering in shock at him.

"He's gone!" Saachi gasped. She was holding the door open.

"Holy shit!" Megan stepped forward and disappeared from Jin's view. She then stepped back out. "He's not in there!"

Mischievously, Jin reached over and tapped Megan on the shoulder. She jumped with a faint shriek. Jin was half in and half out of the doorway.

"Half your body is missing!" Saachi said, gawking.

"Hey, what are you doing over there?" a new voice shouted at them.

Mina shoved Jin through the door and closed it.

From the other side, Jin could hear Mina and her friends explaining that they'd thought it was the restroom. As they were escorted away, Mina turned and waved goodbye.

Elated, Jin watched from the other side of the door. He realized he'd forgotten to tell the professors about the portal. Maybe this was the answer they were looking for.

CHAPTER 19

Evil Dr. Vance

Sunday, May 4

Jin walked to the front of the Book Nook, grabbed a novel off an end table that said NEW BOOKS, and hopped on the line for the cash register. Lucia, the owner, smiled in surprise as she rang him up.

"I didn't see you come in," she said. "You must have snuck right by me."

"Just came in for a book," Jin said. Only then did he notice that the book he had grabbed was a historical romance.

Lucia winked as she bagged his purchase. "I wouldn't have picked you as a Regency romance type of reader."

Blushing, he thanked her, took his bag, and quickly left the store. He wondered if Mina might like the book he'd just bought. He decided he would bring it to her the next time he saw her. Before he left the shopping center, he remembered his promise to Sam and his brother. He stopped by Bread &

Butter, which was three stores down from the Book Nook. At the register, he spotted a box full of individually wrapped brownies and thought of how much Mina loved them, and he grabbed a brownie for her and one for himself as he ordered.

A sweet to remind him of his sweetheart. Jin grinned to himself.

After paying for the food, he pulled his cap down low and rushed over to Sam's building and texted his friend. At the garage door, Joey was already waiting to let him in. They went upstairs and spread out the food on the dining table.

"Now that you're back, you gonna tell me who you were meeting?" Sam asked.

"I was meeting a girl I really like," Jin admitted.

"Name, photo, age, and does she have any cute friends?"

From his wallet, Jin pulled out the first Polaroid Mina had given him and showed it to Sam.

Sam whistled. "She's gorgeous! When do we get to meet her and her friends?"

"Hey, do me a favor and keep this between us for now," Jin said. "I don't feel like talking about her to everyone."

"It's cool," Sam replied. "I understand."

Joey looked at the photo and nodded in approval. "She's really pretty, Jin. But I wouldn't introduce her friends to my creepy brother. She might break up with you for having bad taste in people."

"Shut up." Sam kicked at Joey under the table.

"You're just too ugly," Joey teased.

As the brothers squabbled, Jin finished up his meal,

grabbed his backpack from Sam's closet, and changed into his black T-shirt.

Outside, the black SUV was waiting in the same spot where it had been before. Jin quickly headed for the bus stop and watched as the car followed him home.

As Jin was walking to his house, a silver Mercedes pulled up alongside him. It was Dr. Vance.

"Jin, get in, we need to talk."

Alarmed, Jin immediately shook his head. He wasn't about to get into a car alone with this man after everything the other Dr. Brennan had said. "My house is a block away and I really need to go home."

Dr. Vance sighed, pulled his car to the curb, and got out to walk over to Jin.

"Okay, let's talk here. Why haven't you called me about my request to come with me to TULLY?"

"I've been studying for my AP tests," Jin replied. "It's been very busy."

"Well, what about your teleporting? Have you even tried to go to the other world?" Dr. Vance asked.

If Dr. Brennan was right, then this was a trick question and Dr. Vance already knew the answer.

"It happened briefly today," Jin lied. "I had no control over it. I was at my friend's house and then I was somewhere else. A deserted world with no people. I was there for less than a minute before I poufed back to my friend's home."

"This is all the more reason for us to go to our research facility at TULLY," Dr. Vance said. He faked a concerned look. "The sooner the better. How about this Saturday? It's a two-hour drive into Virginia. We'll need the whole day."

The other Dr. Brennan's words played in Jin's head, making him angry. How dare this man want to lock him away!

"Why do I need to go?" Jin asked.

"Because I think the answer to your dilemma can be found in my laboratory," Dr. Vance said. "Tundra Labs is a multibillion-dollar state-of-the-art laboratory where we can examine you and the phenomenon better."

Examine him? That set off alarm bells in Jin's head. It made him feel like a lab rat.

"If you come to the labs, we can find a solution that can help you," Dr. Vance continued. "You don't want to be glitching in and out of your world the rest of your life. It's not safe. What if you're suddenly teleported into a world that's uninhabitable to humans? It could kill you in less than a minute."

Dr. Vance's words made Jin pause. It was a fear that the other Dr. Brennan had mentioned also. But as Jin saw it, his teleportation had always been linked to his emotions. When he felt all alone and thought he could never see Mina again, he went to the world devoid of humans. When he was angry and frustrated with Mina, he went to the military world with curfews and scary patrolmen. There was a correlation. Even if he wasn't sure about it, he believed that if he could control his emotions, he could control where he was sent. However, he was not going to let Dr. Vance know any of this. He didn't trust Dr. Vance at all.

"Now's not a great time," Jin said. "My parents would never let me go on a trip during AP tests."

"It will only take a day," Dr. Vance said.

"Yeah, but I still have several APs to study for," Jin replied.

"I think it's in your best interests to go this weekend—"

"I'm telling you no! I don't want to." Jin cut Dr. Vance off.

Jin caught a glimpse of intense rage before Dr. Vance masked it. "Is there something going on that you haven't told me about?"

Suddenly furious himself, Jin went on the attack. "Tell you the truth, Dr. Vance, you are starting to piss me off. You broke into my house while my parents were out. You took my blood and examined me like a monkey in a cage. There's a black SUV that's following me around everywhere. And you talk about me like I'm an alien specimen you need to dissect. You're really freaking me out! So no, I don't want to go to your lab and be examined."

Dr. Vance sneered for a split second before he schooled his expression to one of pretend understanding.

"Jin, I'm so sorry, I had no idea I was making you feel this way," he said. "I didn't break into your house. Like I told you, the door was left ajar. I would have just closed it and left, but I heard you, so I decided to go inside. In hindsight, that was a poor choice on my part."

There was no way the door had been ajar. Jin's front door was self-locking and so heavy that it slammed even if it was opened a little. It was why his whole family had gotten into the habit of shutting the door gently. That day, his parents had left in a rush and Jin had heard the slamming of the door. The professor was lying.

"I'm sorry you thought I was creepy. I don't have the best bedside manner, which is why I'm not a practicing medical doctor," Dr. Vance continued with his insincere smile. "I have no idea why a strange car is following you around, but are you sure it's following *you*? This is Washington, DC. There are many politicians and diplomats living right in your neighborhood. It might just seem like they're targeting you. But I'm sure if you really think about it, you'll realize they aren't always around. I think you've been watching too many spy movies."

He's gaslighting me, Jin thought. *He knows I know he's tailing me.*

This was exactly why it would do no good to tell anyone about Dr. Vance's plans. Who in their right mind would believe anything Jin said against a Tundra Labs director? No, the only thing Jin could do was protect himself.

"And as for treating you like a lab rat, for that I truly apologize, Jin. I am a research professor and an awkward nerd." Dr. Vance smiled self-deprecatingly. "I would never intentionally do anything that makes you feel uncomfortable. Trust me. I only have your best interests at heart."

I don't trust you.

"Well, I'll talk to my parents about going to the lab," Jin said. "I'm sure one of them will want to come with me; they're kind of overprotective. But it wouldn't be until after graduation. There's a lot of stuff going on at school. And I have prom and graduation coming."

Dr. Vance's face contorted in fury. Now he wasn't even trying to hide it.

"Besides, I haven't seen the anomaly in a while now," Jin continued. "Maybe it stopped and it's no longer an issue anymore."

"Highly doubtful," Dr. Vance said. "What's more likely is that it has gone dormant and will reappear when you least expect it. But I'll respect your wishes for now. Contact me as soon as it happens again."

As Dr. Vance moved to enter his car, Jin asked, "Have you talked with Dr. Brennan? Is he all right?"

"Dr. Brennan? I'm sure he's fine," the man replied as he got into his car and drove away.

Jin was sure he wasn't.

CHAPTER 20

Just a Regular Old Date

Tuesday, May 6

The past few days had been unseasonably cold for early May, but no one was complaining. At least it was dry and sunny. The severe storms had died down across the globe, and people were praying that the good weather would hold. Everyone was sick and tired of rain. Jin was sure that going through the portal had made a difference, and he planned on using it again to see Mina.

Heading out to his AP Psychology test in the early morning, Jin stepped outside and immediately caught sight of the black SUV. The front door opened.

"Jin, come back! I'll give you a ride to school," Phil said.

With a sigh of relief, Jin went back inside.

After he turned in his exam, he headed to Sam's apartment. This time he didn't bother to try to ditch the men following him. He entered the building by helping an elderly woman with her shopping cart and then took the elevator straight to the garage, where he immediately snuck out the door.

At the Book Nook, he rushed to the back room and immediately entered Wordplay. His watch said 11:55. Not seeing Mina in the store yet, he went to the café and snagged a chair near the far window. A few minutes later, he saw Mina crossing the street, punctual as always. She seemed lost in her thoughts, her face furrowed with anxiety. As soon as she spotted him in the window, she smiled, but Jin could see the fear she was trying to hide.

"Did you tell your parents about the professor? Did you report him to the police? Should I text the professors?" She asked her questions all at once as she gave him a big hug.

"No, I didn't because no one would believe me," Jin replied. "But don't worry, I won't ever be alone with him again. And don't text them. Today, we're not seeing the professors. We're just going to go on a date. No talk of the other world. No talk of the professors or Tundra Labs. Just a regular old date."

Mina frowned, her eyebrows scrunched up.

Jin gently rubbed at the furrows between her brows and smiled down at her.

"Let's be a normal couple today, okay?"

Leaning against Jin's chest, Mina released a deep breath and nodded.

"Where do you want to go?" he asked.

She looked up at him with a shy smile. "I know the perfect spot!"

Mina called for a cab and they went to the National

Gallery of Art. The large marble west building, with its neoclassical design and tall columns, was beautiful and a sharp contrast with the very modern, pristine, boxy look of the east building.

"This is my favorite place in DC," Mina said. "I used to come here all the time with my mom."

"Which building are we going to?" Jin asked.

Mina pulled him toward the west building. "Hi, my name is Mina and I'll be your tour guide today."

They walked through the galleries one by one, enjoying the beauty of the paintings, until they reached the west garden court in the atrium at the end of the main-floor corridor. It was like walking into a private indoor park filled with trees yet enclosed by marble columns. They walked past a beautiful fountain adorned with statues that puzzled Jin.

"Are those cupids strangling a bird?"

Mina giggled. "They're cherubs, and they're supposed to be playing with the swan."

Jin looked dubious. "That swan is not happy."

"These fountains are from King Louis the Fourteenth's château at Versailles. He was known for extreme ostentation."

"Was that the one that got guillotined?"

"No, that was Louis the Sixteenth. This one called himself the Sun King."

Jin looked around the garden room. "I remember coming here with you and our moms. I'm pretty sure I was crying."

"You were such a crybaby all the time," Mina retorted.

Just then, he had a memory of little Mina waving a huge dead bug in his face and chasing him around the fountain.

"Cicadas!" Jin said accusingly. "That was the year we had

all the cicadas, and I hated them. But you would keep them in your pocket and chase me with them!"

Mina began to laugh. "You were scared of everything."

"I still have a bug phobia because of you!"

"How's that my fault?" Mina asked in wide-eyed innocence.

Shaking his head, he glared at her accusingly. "What kid collects dead bugs?"

"Why not? Cicadas are cool-looking," Mina responded.

They were walking past a row of large plants when Mina flicked a leaf toward Jin, yelling, "Watch out! A bug!"

Jin flinched and then glowered at Mina.

"Now I'm remembering how you were always terrorizing me," he accused her.

"It was too easy," she said with a big grin. "Do you remember how our moms would take us to all the museums?"

"My favorite was the natural history museum," Jin remembered. "I loved that elephant in the rotunda."

"You were scared of it," Mina retorted.

"No, I wasn't!"

"Yes, you would always cry when you saw it."

"It's because I was sad that it was dead. Not that I was afraid of it."

"Sure, whatever you say." Mina steered him toward the exit.

"I'm telling you I wasn't scared," Jin complained.

Outside the museum, they came across a line of food trucks on Constitution Ave. Jin looked at Mina and saw her eyes light up.

"Hungry?"

Mina immediately pointed to a black food truck with a big sign that said ASTRO DOUGHNUTS AND FRIED CHICKEN.

"I've always wanted to try them," she said. Mina headed toward the truck but halted when Jin stopped walking. Mina used both her hands to pull Jin forward, but he didn't budge. He planted his feet firmly and made himself as heavy as possible.

"That sounds unhealthy," he said. He pointed at a food truck with vegetables in their logo called Salad Thyme. "How about that one? I bet they have much healthier options."

Mina gave him the stink eye and turned her face as far away as she could while still clinging to his arm. Chuckling, he spun her around into his embrace.

"I'm kidding, we'll get whatever you want," he said.

They ordered two huge crème brûlée donuts dripping with glaze and a four-piece order of fried chicken with Tater Tots, coleslaw, and a large lemonade. Jin grabbed their cartons of food and drink while Mina paid, her left hand clinging to the crook of his elbow.

"Where should we go to eat all this?" he asked.

"I know the best picnic spot," Mina said. She guided him to the corner. They crossed Seventh Street and entered the National Gallery of Art's sculpture park. She made a beeline for a stone seat in front of a large mosaic on a free-standing wall. A few rays of sunlight shone through the leaves and hit the glass and colored stones of the mural, dazzling them with the shimmer of turquoises, golds, and corals.

"Wow! What is that?" Jin asked.

"This is called *Orphée*, by Marc Chagall," Mina replied. "It was a gift he made for his friends the Nefs. My mom loved it. She and Aunt Jackie would walk down the Nefs' street in Georgetown just to get a glimpse of it over the garden wall.

When the Nefs died, they gifted it to the National Gallery. I remember how excited our moms were to see it again, not in a private garden, but in a public display. Aunt Jackie and I come here every year on my mom's birthday and have a little picnic. This year, for the first time, my dad joined us!"

"When was your mom's birthday?"

"April fifth," Mina replied. She seemed lost in a wonderful memory. "It was perfect picnic weather, not too cold, not too hot. My mom would have loved it. There's this Japanese word that she taught me. *Komorebi.* It's when you see sunlight filtered through leaves. And that day the light rays that peeked through the canopy were dancing and reflecting off the mural. It was as if Mom was with us."

"I wish I'd been there," Jin said.

"Me too."

"You know, I've been to the sculpture garden in my world, but I don't recall seeing the mural there," Jin said.

"Strange, but I wonder if it's because they moved it here after you went to your world," Mina said. Her brow furrowed in concern. "But I know it has to be there. It's a Chagall mural. Maybe you can look it up?"

"Sure, but now, let's eat!"

When they were done, they walked around the rest of the garden, rediscovering the art they remembered from when they were younger.

"The typewriter eraser seemed a lot bigger when we were little," Jin stated.

"At least it was kind of funny-looking. I hated the headless children statues," Mina replied.

"I didn't like the spider . . ."

"What? But the spider's so cool!"

"It's freaky!"

They bickered amicably as they wandered the entire garden park and then exited right where they had entered. Immediately, Mina pointed at the ice cream truck across the street.

"Are you a bottomless pit? Do you ever get full?"

"I have a second stomach for dessert," Mina said. "Besides, I have a very fast metabolism. And you ate just as much as I did."

"But I'm a lot bigger than you."

"So what you're saying is we should get some funnel cake too, am I right?"

Jin groaned. "You sure you don't have a tapeworm in you?"

As wonderful as their date was, Jin found himself exhausted and dragging. His hand shook as he glanced at his watch and saw that he'd spent nearly five hours in Mina's world.

"This was the best date ever," Mina said with a wistful smile. "I wish we could spend longer, but my dad wants to go out for dinner tonight. He's taking me to Korean barbecue in Virginia."

"That sounds great," Jin said, hiding his trembling left hand from Mina. He didn't want her to see how bad he felt.

"I wish you could come," Mina said.

"Me too." Jin hugged her, resting his cheek on her head. "When do we meet next?"

"I'm only taking one AP test on Thursday," Mina said.

"I'm done Friday," Jin said. "Let's meet then."

"Same time?" she asked.

"Cool!"

Mina looked around and could see that the DC rush hour was in full swing.

"We can walk over to Chinatown and take the Metro home," she said, pointing across Constitution.

At that moment, Jin could see that his trembling hand had turned translucent. He was beginning to disappear. He wasn't going to make it back to the bookstore. Sliding his hand behind his back, he smiled down at her.

"Mina, I should go now," he told her gently. "I think five hours might be the limit of how long I can stay."

Disappointment crossed her face before she nodded. "Of course. It's been a long day. You must be tired."

Jin gave her a sweet kiss and studied her face, as if to memorize it. "I love you."

"I love you too," she said. And then she let go.

Jin teleported into his world at the same corner, Seventh and Constitution, right across from the park. He immediately felt better. He went into the sculpture park to look for the Chagall mural. There were only ten minutes left before the park closed. He sprinted to the corner where the mural had been. But the wall was gone. Instead, there was a series of various-sized stones, arranged in a haphazard manner. What had happened to the mural?

Walking to the Metro station, he thought of Mina making this same walk, but in her world. He wondered how many other things had changed between their worlds. Once on the Metro, he looked up the Chagall mural on his cell phone and found an article that explained that it had been sold to a private collector.

What a shame, he thought. *Mina would be so disappointed to hear this news.*

Getting off the Metro, Jin realized he had forgotten to return to Sam's building. The SUV men would realize that he had snuck by them at some point.

Let them sit there all night, he thought with a snicker.

CHAPTER 21

All Alone with Mina

Wednesday, May 7

The next morning, Jin woke up to a violent storm. His heart sank with guilt. If only he'd used the portal to return to his world. Regret coursed through him as lightning strikes illuminated his dark room.

Downstairs, his parents were watching the morning news as they drank their coffee.

"I guess all that lovely weather was too good to last," Alice sighed.

"Jin, it would be best to stay in today if you can," Phil said.

"I'm just studying anyway," Jin replied. Curious to see if the men following him were still parked outside his house, he peered out the front window. The rain was too thick and hard to see through, but he didn't think he saw a black SUV. Maybe they'd given up trying to follow him today because of the weather.

Several hours later, Jin received a call on his cell phone. A feeling of dread tingled in his stomach when he saw that the number was from Tundra Labs. At first, he ignored the call, but when his phone kept ringing, he finally answered it.

"Jin, this is Dr. Vance. I see you've been traveling again," the doctor said. "I think we can no longer delay. I'm afraid I will have to insist that you come with me to TULLY as soon as possible."

"No, Dr. Vance, I have no obligation to go with you," Jin replied. "I would prefer that you leave me alone."

"I am trying to help you, young man," Dr. Vance sputtered.

"I asked Dr. Brennan for help, not you," Jin said. "I don't want anything from you."

He hung up the phone, his heart racing with adrenaline. There was no way this would stop Dr. Vance from harassing him, but at least he wouldn't have to pretend anymore.

Friday, May 9

"Jin, come eat," Alice called up.

Alice had made him a breakfast of champions. Pancakes and bacon and scrambled eggs and hash browns. There was so much food Jin was shocked.

"Who's all this food for?" he asked.

"It's all for me, you can't have any," his sister Meredith said as she came down the stairs.

"Hey! When'd you get here?"

"Late last night! I took my last final, and since the rest are papers, I came home!" She plopped down at the kitchen table and raised an eyebrow as she gave him the once-over. "Why are you dressed like you're going on a date?"

Jin shrugged. He'd wanted to impress Mina and was wearing a black linen bomber jacket over a white T-shirt and dark jeans. Fortunately, the storm had subsided. It was now raining lightly, which was a huge relief. Using the portal was clearly not as disruptive as teleporting. This was a good reminder that when returning, he needed to get to the portal before he became physically depleted, because that was best for his world.

"Do you have a date?" Meredith asked suspiciously.

"We're taking club photos," Jin replied. There was no way he would tell Meredith anything. When she was curious, she was like a pit bull in attack mode. She would never let it go.

"What did you do with all your stuff from school?" he asked.

"Dad made me put it all in storage," she said.

Meredith began shoveling huge bites of pancake into her mouth.

"Try to take human bites, ya animal," Jin said in disgust.

"Go step on a Lego," Meredith retorted as maple syrup dripped down her chin.

"After you get a paper cut between your fingers," Jin replied.

"I hope your phone dies before you can charge it."

"I hope your charger works only when you hold it at a weird angle."

"I hope you run out of toilet paper in a public bathroom."

"I hope you fall into a public toilet while peeing."

"I hope your bread is always moldy."

"I hope your toothbrush is always wet."

Meredith cackled, letting pancake crumbs fly all over the table.

"That's so gross," Jin said. "But I still win."

Whatever his issues about his adoption might have been, he appreciated that Meredith and Jane had always treated him like a member of the family when they'd been just children themselves. He refused to say he was lucky. Losing his world could never be categorized as lucky. But it could have been worse. And he was thankful that it wasn't.

The conversation turned to school as he asked his sister how her semester had gone. Finishing his plate, he got ready to leave.

"Good luck on your test, Jin," Alice said.

"Thanks, Mom." Jin grinned. He waved at his sister and went downstairs.

"I hope you step in a dirty puddle with your socks on!" Meredith yelled after him.

Jin laughed as he went out the front door.

The first thing he did was look for the black SUV. Relieved that there was no sign of it, he rushed to school.

After his exam, Jin headed straight for Spring Valley shopping center. At the Book Nook, he bought another pretty drawing journal and a box of chocolates for Mina. Lucia greeted Jin warmly.

"You've become quite the regular here," she said as she bagged his purchase and placed his receipt in his shopping bag.

"I like bookstores," he replied.

"I'm so glad to hear that," she said. "Thank you for your support!"

Once she turned her attention to the next shopper, he

snuck to the back of the store and went through the portal door. When he looked around, the first thing he noticed was Lucia talking to some booksellers in the café area. It boggled his mind to have left one Lucia, only to meet another one a few seconds later.

A large clock above the front entrance showed that it was exactly noon. From the window, he caught sight of Mina walking into Wordplay wearing a T-shirt and jean shorts. Her face lit up when she saw him. He knew he would never get tired of seeing her this way. Happy to see him. To spend time with him. He ached with the need to be a part of her world. As hard as it was to leave behind his friends and family, he would do so to be with her. Because it felt right. The portal was the key to seeing Mina and still not harming his world. He was so grateful for its existence. He knew it had to be the answer to his problem.

"Are we going to see the professors today?" she asked. "They've been wanting to talk to you."

Jin shook his head. He wanted to be completely selfish. His last date with Mina had left him hungry for more time alone with her.

Mina glared at him and was just about to argue when Jin placed a gentle finger on her lips. "I just want to have another romantic date with you."

Because I might never have this chance again.

She reluctantly agreed and was letting him lead her toward the exit when they were stopped by Lucia, the owner.

"Oh, hey, I almost named this store Book Nook," Lucia said as she stared down at Jin's shopping bag. "I loved it, but my wife told me this space was too big to be a nook."

It was a surreal experience to speak to Lucia about a store

that was still hers, but in another world. Jin shook off the feeling and smiled.

"I think Wordplay is great," he replied. "It really suits this store."

"I agree," Lucia said. "And I wouldn't give up this place for anything. This was my dream for such a long time. But it's just nice to see there's a bookstore out there called Book Nook. It makes me happy."

Jin wondered what had happened between the worlds that had changed Book Nook to Wordplay. Lucia had achieved what she wanted to do here. In his world, she only dreamed of it. Since learning about the split in the timeline, Jin had thought of it as him being given life in exchange for the loss of something else. In Jin's life, the split had left him without his birth mom and Mina. But maybe it hadn't affected just him. After all, Dr. Brennan had lost Dr. Prescott, and Lucia had settled for the smaller Book Nook when she'd dreamed of a large bookstore and café. Maybe the split forced people to make some kind of choice, and in his world, they chose caution.

"Oh, look! I want chocolates!" Mina had stopped in front of a large display of chocolate in fancy gold boxes.

"No, you can't have that," Jin said sternly.

"Why not?" Mina sulking was delightfully cute to Jin. She stuck her lower lip so far out her upper lip disappeared.

"Because I already bought you some." Jin handed the Book Nook bag of chocolates to her. "But you have to eat them later. Let's go grab lunch now."

"I know just the place!" Mina crowed in happiness.

Exiting the bookstore, Jin was struck by how much warmer it was in Mina's world.

"You look nice, but aren't you hot?" Mina asked.

Jin nodded. He took off his jacket while trying to keep hold of Mina's hand.

"Is the weather supposed to be this hot here?" he said. "It's much colder at home."

"It's definitely hotter than usual," Mina said. "I'm really not fond of hot weather."

"Well, I'm enjoying it," Jin teased.

Mina smacked Jin hard on the shoulder. "Creep."

They walked for several blocks until they reached a small restaurant called Zen's Chicken next to a grocery store.

"This is my favorite Korean fried chicken," Mina said.

"We don't have this at home," Jin remarked. "I'm pretty sure it's a Tex-Mex place called Guadalupe's."

"That's so funny! This was previously Auntie Rosa's until just a few months ago. It wasn't very good Tex-Mex."

"Neither is Guadalupe's!"

"I wish my mom had seen Zen's open," Mina sighed. "My grandparents used to own a fried chicken franchise in Korea. My mom wanted to open one here with my grandma's special spicy sauce. She thought it would do well."

Jin thought about all the food options back home. To be honest, he'd never heard of Korean fried chicken. But he didn't say anything to Mina, not wanting to seem less Korean than he already felt.

"Your grandparents live in Korea, right?"

"Yeah, and since they're older it's been harder for them to come visit," Mina said. "But my dad said I'm going to Korea this summer to stay with them! I'm really excited about it. I wish you could go with me."

"Me too," Jin replied.

Before they could get too melancholy, the food arrived, and Jin was shocked at the amount Mina had ordered.

"How many chickens did you order, Mina?"

"Well, I had to get the original so you can taste how good it is, then I got the honey garlic 'cause it's sweet and spicy, and the spicy, which is my favorite," Mina explained. "And I had to get some tteokbokki, which is a must with Korean fried chicken. I got the rosé version because it's a little milder."

"I don't think I've ever had any of this before," Jin said. "What is that?"

He pointed at the tteokbokki.

Mina blinked at him in disbelief. "Oh, you poor thing, you haven't lived."

Using her chopsticks, she grabbed a piece of rice cake and stuck it in his mouth. "The regular version is just gochujang spicy. But this has milk and cheese in it to make it more mellow."

"Wow! That's amazing!" Jin said. He picked up his chopsticks and speared his own rice cakes.

"Don't stab your food, that's bad manners," Mina chided Jin.

"Really? I didn't know that."

Mina looked at him puzzled. "Didn't you say your adopted parents took you to Korean restaurants often?"

"Restaurant," Jin corrected. "Singular. As in the only one they know and like. And it's all the way out in Annandale, Virginia."

"Aren't there a lot of Korean restaurants in Annandale?"

"Yes, but they only go to the one right off the beltway.

Seoul Palace. They've never actually gone into Annandale to see what else is there. I think they're a bit uncomfortable."

"I'm sorry you didn't have anyone to show you your Korean heritage," Mina said.

That was the other big thing Jin had lost in his world. The ability to connect with his cultural roots. It left a bitter ball of resentment that stuck in his throat, like a fish bone he couldn't dislodge. There was no one to blame, so he pointed it inward.

"But it's never too late." Mina smiled. She served him a piece of spicy fried chicken. "Eat this!"

Jin gave Mina a dubious glance. "I'm not sure fried chicken is actually culturally Korean."

"You're right, it's soul food and South Koreans learned how to make it from Black American soldiers stationed there during the Korean War. But then they added Korean-style sauces and it became a Korean craze. And *now* it's part of our shared cultural heritage." Mina beamed at him.

They ate until they were stuffed.

"Midnight snack," Mina said as she boxed up the leftovers. "Next time, I want to take you to this awesome ramen shop not too far from school," she continued. "We can go tomorrow. I have no plans."

Jin hesitated.

"Is that too soon? Will it cause problems in your world?" she asked.

"I don't know, but I want to be cautious. I would see you every day if I could," Jin said.

"I know," Mina sighed. "So let's meet Monday at noon. School's out for seniors anyway."

Jin agreed and looked at his watch. Only two hours had passed, and he was still feeling good.

"Where should we go next on our date?"

He watched as Mina opened up the box of chocolates he'd given her and quickly devoured two pieces.

"My dad is in New York today for work, let's go hang out at my house," she offered.

He'd been about to tease her about the melted chocolate on her lips, but his words dried up at her suggestion. All alone with Mina. He nodded.

Jin entered Mina's town house with some hesitancy. This was the actual place he used to visit every day with his mother. Unlike the version of Mina's house in his world, this home felt warm and lived-in. Mina's mom's artwork was hung all around the house, vibrant and beautiful. He could still see her in his memories, always smiling and giving him big hugs. So vivid was the memory that he almost expected Aunt Emma to pop out of the kitchen and offer him something to eat. Sitting down in the living room, he caught sight of a familiar figure in the glass display case.

"Hey, that's the little robot you made!"

"Yeah, Bomi, my little buddy," Mina answered. "He's just a statue here, but I'm glad I still have him."

Mina got a phone call, which she didn't answer. And then another call, which she also ignored.

"Shouldn't you answer that?" Jin asked.

"It's just my dad checking up on me," she said. "I don't want to talk to him right now."

She pulled on Jin's arm. "Come on. Let's go up to my room."

Jin felt uncomfortably warm. His heart pounded loud

and tight in his chest. He let her lead him upstairs to her room. The click of the door behind them caused a rush of blood to his head, making him slightly dizzy. Mina flopped down on the bed first and pulled him next to her.

"I've been dreaming of you every night," she whispered.

Jin couldn't respond. He had no words. He lost himself in brown eyes that were focused solely on him.

"Do you hold on to me in your dreams also?" he asked.

"Always."

"Then don't ever let go."

She pulled herself closer, her body molding against his. He could only swallow in response. And then she kissed him.

This kiss was nothing like all the ones that had come before it. It was an eruption of heat and a longing so intense that his mind was lost in the sensations of Mina. The fullness of her lips, the sweetness of her mouth, her arms embracing him tight. He could no longer distinguish her heartbeat from his. His breathing turned ragged and harsh and his fingers trembled as they glided through her hair and down her back. He couldn't think of anything but the touch and smell and taste of Mina.

From downstairs they heard the front door slam and a man's voice.

"Mina, are you home? I came back early from NY," Mina's dad yelled. "I got Korean fried chicken!"

"Oh my god!" Mina bolted upright. In her panic, she jumped out of bed. The next minute Jin was on the floor of a completely unfurnished room, all by himself.

CHAPTER 22

Kidnapped!

Friday, May 9

The room was dark but not as dusty as it should have been. Jin slowly made his way downstairs, sad to know that Mina's house was empty once again. He walked by the room that was Aunt Emma's studio. He had happy memories of sitting on the rug playing with Mina, watching Aunt Emma paint. She would always sketch little doodles of them that made them laugh. Their moms loved cooking together. If his mom made galbi-jjim, his favorite stewed meat dish, then Aunt Emma would make all the vegetable side dishes. They were always doing things together. He missed them both.

Walking to the front door, he stopped and looked down at his feet. He'd left his shoes and jacket in Mina's world. He wondered how Mina would explain them to her father. Knowing her, she'd probably say she'd stolen them. Jin chuckled at the thought and then frowned when he realized it was raining outside and all he had were socks.

He remembered Meredith yelling at him, *I hope you step in a dirty puddle with your socks on!*

"Ugh, this is all your fault, Meredith! You cursed me."

Hoping for a miracle, he peeked into the coat closet to see if there was anything he could use and was psyched to see a pair of house slippers left on the floor. They were black, rubber, and open-toed. No use against the rain, but they would keep him from stepping on a nail or glass and having to get a tetanus shot.

Putting on the slippers, he opened the door and bolted out of the house. The rain pelted him as he made his way home. It was pulsing and heavy; he couldn't even look up at the sky to see if the anomaly was there. Turning onto his street, Jin noticed a gray sedan parked on the corner with its windshield wipers on. He could make out two men just sitting inside.

One of the men caught Jin looking and turned away. Jin didn't recognize either of them, but they were definitely Tundra men. Shivering from the cold, he entered his house and raced quickly into a hot shower.

Saturday, May 10

The next morning, Jin woke to booming thunder that sounded like it was inside the house. Climbing out of bed, he went over to the window and saw what looked like a river of rainwater rushing through the streets. The weather was the worst it had been since the first time Jin had taken note of the anomalies. The sky was filled with dark gray clouds that rolled and billowed violently. He huddled under a blanket in his room as the temperature dropped so low that what should have been a warm May day felt arctic. It reminded him of the nightmare he'd just had.

In his dream, he was in an apocalyptic movie, alone in a world that was all red skies and fire burning everything around him. To wake up to a scene the exact opposite of what he'd just envisioned was ironic and horrifying.

This couldn't be the end of his world. It was too soon.

And then the power went out. Jin ran downstairs. His parents were checking the pantry.

"I'll start the generator as soon as this rain stops," Phil said.

"Jin, can you bring up some bottles of water from the garage?" Alice asked. "There's a warning not to drink the water because of contamination."

"Mom! Dad! Jin!" Meredith yelled as she pounded down the stairs. "Anyone have a portable charger? My phone died before I could plug it in."

Their lack of alarm made Jin breathe a little easier.

"I have one, I'll get it after I go to the garage for Mom," Jin replied.

"What the hell is wrong with this weather?" Meredith asked. "There's some creepy cult that's been posting about doomsday and how it's the end times."

"The weather has been quite ominous," Alice replied. "It's actually quite frightening."

Jin felt a needling pain at their words. Twice now he had left Mina's world without using the portal. It was his fault that the weather was dangerous. Or was it?

No one knew what it would look like if the two worlds merged. Dr. Brennan and Dr. Prescott both seemed to think such a merge was probable but had no idea of what would actually happen to him. He looked at his adopted family and worried about what would happen to them, especially his dad.

Beloved pediatric oncologist Dr. Philip Joseph Kanter passed away on October 27 of this year.

Just as with Jin, there was no Phil Kanter in Mina's world to merge with. It was frightening to think about what could happen. Jin had no way of knowing if they would even be conscious of such an event. Whether it would be a fade-to-black moment as one world was subsumed by the other or if they would be completely unaware of it happening. They could simply disappear. He turned his mind away from the painful thought. But he was plagued with further questions.

He thought of Alice, his sisters Meredith and Jane, and all of his friends. If this world disappeared, what physically happened to everyone? Did their bodies vanish, leaving only consciousnesses to merge? Would anyone be aware of what was happening? So many questions that no one had answers to because no one had ever gone through anything like this.

Jin was fast coming to the realization that nobody could help him. He had no hope that the professors could find a solution. No matter what they said, the answer was not going to be in science. He knew the answer had to be in the portal at the bookstore. It was the only place where he could exist in both worlds without any effort. It was his safe haven. He was sure it meant that there was a way for him to safely cross over. But he couldn't live in a bookstore forever. There had to be more to the solution. He just didn't know what it was.

Sunday, May 11

The rain didn't stop all weekend, making it harder for the electric company to fix the record number of power outages. Unfortunately, Phil couldn't use their outdoor generator because of the rain. All DC residents were warned not to drink or cook with the water and advised to stay inside. The weather was too dangerous for driving. No restaurants were open. School was canceled and the remaining AP exams rescheduled. Jin felt crushed. He hated that his selfish actions were affecting everyone. He hated feeling guilty all the time.

"Happy Mother's Day," Jin said to Alice as they gathered around the dining room table for a makeshift brunch. He passed her a gift bag of her favorite skin care products. "I'm sorry we couldn't go out for a nice meal."

"This is perfectly fine." Alice smiled. "I'm happy we're all safe here together!"

"Good thing I bought the cupcakes yesterday or we'd be celebrating with Oreos!" Meredith said as she passed everyone red velvet cupcakes from their mother's favorite bakery.

"I like Oreos!" Phil retorted. "But you do deserve better than this, my love! And we will make it up to you after Jane comes home."

Thunder cracked loudly nearby, causing all of them to jump and then laugh in relief.

While Meredith, Phil, and Alice crowded together around the fireplace in the family room, Jin took a battery-powered LED lantern up to the loft. With the rain pelting against the glass doors, the dim light of the little lantern, and the cold chill permeating the house, it was like he was camping in the wilderness. Even knowing his family was two floors down, Jin felt completely alone.

Mark texted in the early afternoon.

Mark: hey you guys okay?

Jin: no power
can't use outdoor generator in rain
totally useless
my sister used all my portable batteries
im on 15%

Mark: come over
we have an indoor generator

Jin: sweet

Jin jumped at the opportunity to leave the house and get away from his thoughts. He grabbed a rain jacket, threw all his electronic items into a backpack, and ran downstairs.

Meredith was sitting in the living room, looking miserable among an array of candles. Alice was knitting next to her, while Phil was on his laptop.

"Where are you going?" Meredith asked.

"Mark's house has an indoor generator, I'm going to go charge my stuff," he said.

"Can you charge mine, please?" she begged piteously, rushing over to hand him her cell phone.

"Wow, I thought this was surgically implanted into your hand," Jin teased.

"You are seeing me at my lowest of lows."

"Don't worry, honey, I rush-ordered an indoor generator. It should arrive tomorrow if we're lucky," Phil said. "Jin, watch out, the roads are very slick and there are trees down all over the place."

As Jin waved goodbye he heard Alice yell, "Be careful! And wear a heavier jacket. It's very cold."

In the foyer, Jin peered outside to see the wind buffeting the treetops but no anomaly in the sky. He pulled on his rain boots, zipped up a warm raincoat over his backpack, and stepped into the pouring rain. Tightening his hood low over his eyes, he began walking to Mark's house. There was hardly anyone outside, and very few cars were on the roads. The danger was from all the debris scattered everywhere, like an obstacle course. The normally fifteen-minute walk took nearly half an hour.

When he got to Mark's house, he was surprised to see that from the outside, the house did not look like it had power. Jin knocked on the door, and Mark immediately greeted him and brought him to the back of the house, where the open kitchen, dining, and family areas were brightly lit up.

"Thanks for letting me come over," Jin said as Mark's parents warmly welcomed him. "My sister Meredith might murder someone if her phone doesn't get charged."

"We can't have that! Happy to have you over," Mr. Henderson said as he shook Jin's hand and Mrs. Henderson gave him a hug.

"Good to see you, Jin! Make yourself at home—as you can see, we're busy cooking. Would you like a snack or drink?"

“No, thank you,” Jin replied politely.

“Come on, let’s go before they make us help them!” Mark said as he pulled Jin down to the basement.

“Lunch will be in an hour!” Mrs. Henderson called after them.

Mark’s dad was a partner at a large law firm, and his mother was a federal judge. They were very low-key and nice people for such a Washington, DC, power couple. But Mark said it was because Jin had never seen them angry.

“Believe me, they are the scariest people,” Mark always said. “You just don’t know their true faces. Hideous.”

The large rec room had a pool table, a large-screen TV, and gaming consoles. It had sliding glass doors that faced a small enclosed backyard.

“We could power the whole house, but my dad said it was a waste of energy,” Mark said. “That’s why they’re only powering a third of the house. The kitchen and the family room for them, and I got the downstairs.”

Mark made himself comfortable in an oversized armchair and picked up a giant bag of cheese puffs. The coffee table was covered with a wide variety of junk food and cookies.

Mark swiped a pair of chopsticks from the table and pointed at a power strip in front of the TV.

“You can use that to charge up,” he said.

Jin opened his bag and gratefully began charging all his electronics. He then watched in fascination as Mark used chopsticks to eat the orange puffs.

“Where’d you learn how to do that?” he asked.

“Diana showed me,” he said. “She learned it from Lauren, who says this is an Asian thing.”

"Ah, I guess I wouldn't know," Jin responded bitterly, sitting on the sofa. "I'm not a real Asian."

His friend looked at him for a long moment before passing him the bag of cheese puffs and a new pair of chopsticks.

"I'm pretty sure this is not going to turn you into a real Asian, but it will keep your fingers from turning orange."

Jin laughed at his friend's wisdom. The problem wasn't not knowing about this little trick, it was feeling like he'd lost out by growing up in a non-Asian family. It was way deeper than cheese puffs but not something he was up to examining right now.

"Can't believe Sam and Liam's neighborhood didn't lose power," Jin said, changing the subject. "Usually, they're the first ones with outages."

"Guess it was our turn," Mark sighed. "But hey, no school, no AP tests. Could be worse."

Jin stilled at Mark's words. His world was colliding with another and he didn't know if he would survive. That was worse.

"There was no school after AP week anyway," Jin retorted. "We're seniors."

"Yeah, but I still had three more AP tests. And now my mom isn't going to force me to make them up because they're being refunded," Mark said. "I win."

A series of beeps came out of Mark's cell phone. When he checked it, he let out a big sigh.

"Man, I'm legit sick of all this rain," he griped. "Diana and her friends are freaking out because they're worried prom will get canceled if this bad weather continues."

Jin smiled weakly. "Can't rain forever."

"Can't go see my girlfriend 'cause she has to stay home

with her family. Can't even play ball at the community center because they lost power too. If you hadn't come over I would've just lost it, I'm so bored."

"What do you want to do?"

"Let's play the new NBA game," Mark replied. "The graphics are killer."

"Before you start your marathon gaming session, come eat," Mark's mother yelled from upstairs. "Jin, you need to help us with all the food we made."

Upstairs, the mouthwatering aroma of shrimp, andouille sausage, and fresh corn bread reminded Jin that he'd only eaten cold cereal and peanut butter and jelly sandwiches the last few days. As he sat next to Mark and devoured the delicious food, he thought about how much Mina would enjoy the meal.

"I never had shrimp and grits this good in my entire life, Mrs. Henderson," Jin raved. "And the corn bread is killer!"

"With the weather keeping us cooped up inside, I went on a cooking frenzy. Please take some corn bread home, Jin. I made a ton!"

"Thank you, I'd love to!"

After spending the afternoon playing video games with Mark and charging up all his devices, including Meredith's phone, Jin packed up his things to take home.

"Looks like it's still real bad out there, you sure you don't want to just sleep over?" Mark asked. "You can stay for dinner. They're cooking up a whole lot of steaks. I think my parents are trying to cook everything in the freezer today."

Although another hot and delicious meal sounded amazing, Jin didn't want to overstay his welcome.

"I would, but Meredith might gnaw off her own arm if I

don't get her phone back to her," he said, sighing. "I'd better get home."

"I don't know, man, it looks even worse now."

They both peered out the window. A heavy mist was rising from the ground even as the rain continued to pound the pavement.

Mark's parents were also concerned. "I wish I could give you a ride home," Mark's father said, "but it's really not safe to drive. I'd feel better if you spent the night. We'll explain to your parents."

"I'll be fine," Jin said. "The roads were pretty empty and the winds have died down. I'll be careful, I promise."

"Here." Mark handed Jin a floppy rain hat. "It's ugly but it will keep the rain off your face. An umbrella would be just useless."

Thanking them for everything, Jin zipped up his raincoat over his precious cargo of charged electronic items, tied the hat over his hood, and left for home. The wind was not as biting as it had been earlier, but halfway through his walk, the rain turned to tiny hail. He was grateful for Mark's hat as he tried to navigate around the debris. As he was about to cross the street, a dark gray sedan suddenly pulled in front of him. Jin froze in shock. Before he could even say a word, two men in black uniforms jumped out and dragged him into the car. One got into the driver's seat while the other shoved Jin into the back seat and got in after him.

"What the hell are you doing?" Jin shouted, fighting hard. The man in the back seat punched him in the face while the driver gunned the engine.

"Get off me!"

Jin struggled against the man, who now had him in a

choke hold. Jin tucked his chin down to keep the man from choking him, locked his elbows, and pushed all his weight on the man's arm. The man pulled a Taser from his jacket, but Jin punched his fist into the man's face and kicked the back of the driver's head hard at the same time. The driver lost control. The car went into a tailspin, crashing into a line of parked cars. Jin swung his whole body toward the door, smashing his captor's head into the window. The man's arms went slack and Jin flung open the door and fell into the street. Seeing that he was only a few blocks from home, he ran as fast as he could, leaving the two unconscious men behind.

"Mom, Dad!" he yelled running into the house. "Help!"

Phil and Alice came down with Meredith fast on their heels.

"What's happened?"

"Oh my gosh, Jin, your face is bleeding!" Alice ran upstairs.

Jin wiped the blood away with the back of his hand.

"These men tried to abduct me in their car," he said. "I fought back and there was a car accident. Come help. They're unconscious."

"Someone call 911," Phil said as he pulled on his shoes and a raincoat.

"I need my phone to call," Meredith said.

Jin took off his coat and backpack and gave the pack to Meredith, who immediately started to look for her phone. Alice reappeared and held some gauze to Jin's cut.

"It's okay, Mom, I'm fine," Jin said as he pushed away the gauze. He led Phil to where the car had crashed, but it was gone. It was now raining lightly.

"I don't understand. They were injured and unconscious!"

Phil was looking at the crushed sides of several of the parked cars as Meredith appeared and called the police.

"This looks like a pretty bad crash, we should get you to the hospital and check you out," Phil said.

Jin shook his head. "I'm fine, the cut is from when he punched me."

"There's a patrol car nearby," Meredith said. "They'll be here in a few minutes."

As they waited for the police to arrive, Meredith took pictures of the accident site while Phil asked for details. The police officer who arrived took the report and the license plates of the damaged parked cars as well as a few other cars in the street.

"We're in luck," the officer said. "Several cars here have dashcams. And that BMW has a clear shot of the whole block. We should be able to get video of the entire accident."

The fact that there might be video evidence came as an enormous relief to Jin. Maybe it would dissuade the Tundra men from escalating their attempts.

"Let's go down to the station. I'll need to get a full incident report," the officer continued.

"Okay, Meredith, you go home and tell your mom what's happened, I'll go with Jin," Phil said.

At the police station, Phil asked for a first aid kit to treat and bandage Jin's wounds while Jin gave a detailed description of the car and the kidnappers.

"I just don't understand how this could happen," Phil said.

"You have no idea who these men were?" the officer asked.

"No, I never saw them before in my life," Jin replied. He

had no intention of telling them about Dr. Vance. Nobody would believe him.

"Well, once we get the footage from the BMW owner and the other cars, we will contact you, but for now you can head home."

When they got home, Alice and Meredith were anxiously waiting to hear the entire story, but Jin was too tired to explain and try to speculate with them about who the kidnappers were. He didn't have the energy, and his entire body was one big throbbing mess. All he wanted to do was sleep.

"If it's okay with you all, I just want to go to my room and crash."

"But what about dinner?" Alice asked.

"I'm not hungry," Jin replied. But that reminded him of the corn bread from Mark's mom. He couldn't believe it was the same day. It felt so long ago. He retrieved it from his backpack and passed it to Meredith. "It's smushed but I bet it's still delicious."

With a tired smile, he dragged himself up to his bedroom. Peeling off his clothes, he could feel the aches and pains he hadn't noticed before and could see new bruises forming. He really needed a shower, but he was too tired and sore to care. He climbed on top of his bedcovers and dreamed of being locked up in a dark cell that kept sinking deeper and deeper into the earth. No matter how much he screamed, no one could hear him.

CHAPTER 23

The Escape

Monday, May 12

The next day, the rains subsided to a drizzle that was cold and miserable but not catastrophic. With school being officially out for seniors, Jin was forced to stay in bed and rest. Luckily, the power returned, but he had to miss his date with Mina because his parents refused to let him leave the house.

"It's too dangerous for you, Jin," Phil said. "We have no information about who these men are or what they wanted. Since there's no school, you have no reason to go anywhere."

Alice and Phil checked on him repeatedly, making sure he was feeling better after his traumatic incident. They were worried about leaving him alone with Meredith, as they were supposed to leave to pick Jane up from Oberlin the following morning.

"He'll be fine! I'll take care of my baby brother," Meredith said.

"I'm a lot bigger than you," he said. "And you can't cook. So who's taking care of who?"

"Hello, delivery, please," Meredith retorted.

"Are restaurants even open yet?" Jin asked.

"We took care of that, Jin. We've got plenty of food in the pantry and we restocked the fridge and the freezer," Phil responded.

"Maybe one of us should stay home," Alice said. "What if the kidnappers come back?"

"I doubt it. The police are patrolling our block," Jin reminded them.

"I've got my papers to write and don't plan to leave the house at all," Meredith chimed in. "I'll make sure to watch over Stink Butt."

Ignoring her insult, Jin said, "Besides, the weather looks good this week and your flights aren't canceled. You need to take advantage of it and help get Jane home."

"They're right, honey," Phil said. "I've told our neighbors to keep an eye on the house. And the police are actively patrolling the neighborhood. They're smart kids. They'll be fine. I'll tell you what, we'll come back in two days instead of three."

"Don't worry, Mom, we'll be safe," Jin insisted.

Tuesday, May 13

His parents left in the early morning for their flight to Cleveland. The plan had been to rent a car at the airport, pack Jane up, and drive her back at a leisurely pace. But they would make the seven-and-a-half-hour drive in one day instead.

Jin woke up at ten a.m. to a text from Meredith.

Meredith: roast beef sandwich in fridge
eat it
don't bother me until dinner

Before he could respond, he received a flurry of text messages in his group chat.

Mark: my moms lost it
been baking cookies all morning
i need you all to come eat them

Liam: on my way

Sam: what kind of cookies?

Mark: peanut butter, oatmeal cranberry, chocolate chip

Jin: im tired

Mark: i don't care
come now

Jin had planned to go see Mina today through the Book Nook. Bringing her some of Mrs. Henderson's delicious cookies would make up for missing her yesterday. Jin hadn't told any of his friends about the attempted abduction, and he'd promised his parents he would stay home. But all he could think about was seeing Mina and the professors and finding a solution to his problem. Jin made up his mind to stop by Mark's place before going to see Mina. He looked out the front window and saw a police car parked at the corner. But then he was stunned to see that the anomaly was back and it had grown again. It no longer looked like it was ripping the sky apart. No, it was as if the anomaly was taking over. Unnerved, he put it out of his mind.

Confident that the Tundra guys wouldn't try again so soon after the first attempt, Jin taped a note on Meredith's door. Pulling on a raincoat, he stepped out into the cold drizzle and started walking to Mark's house. He was only a few blocks from home when he heard the sudden acceleration and the squeal of brakes. He wheeled around and barely managed to jump aside as a black SUV pulled up next to him and the passenger-side door was flung open. As a brawny man in a suit and tie got out of the car, Jin immediately began to run—and then felt something sharp hit the back of his neck. An intense searing pain like a bolt of lightning surged through his body. Going rigid, Jin fell to the ground face-first, spasms jerking his body around as if he was a marionette. Unable to move, he couldn't stop the man who'd tased him from tossing him into the SUV like a sack of rice. Jin gasped as he tried to breathe through the seizures. When the pain finally stopped, Jin's limbs were too weak for him to even sit up and all he could do was breathe harshly.

"Where are you taking me?" he asked, his voice hoarse.

The men didn't answer. Several minutes passed before Jin was able to sit up and look out the window. He recognized the route they were taking. They were on a side street headed for 395 south toward Virginia. Trying not to panic, Jin thought of Mina and how upset she would be with him if he was taken to TULLY. The moment the thought passed through his mind, Jin's stomach lurched as he found himself falling into the road and hitting the curb between two parked cars. Shocked, he recognized that he had just teleported into Mina's world and was on the same street that they had been passing in the SUV. Here the streets were dry and the sun was bright overhead. He was as weak as a baby, but he knew he had to move now. He got up on shaky legs and immediately ran as fast as he could away from where he'd teleported. Looking around as he kept moving, he didn't see Mina anywhere. That meant he only had a minute before he would be pulled back into his world.

Up ahead, Jin spotted a CVS on the next block. Though he felt like puking and all his muscles were sore and painful, he bolted toward the store. He had to make it inside. Running to the door, he hesitated for a brief moment. He wasn't familiar with this neighborhood—he could only hope that this was a CVS in his world also. The door slid open and Jin stepped inside just as he felt the stomach-lurching jump back to his world.

He was now inside a busy fast-food restaurant. The aroma of fried chicken and oil assaulted his nose. He quickly pulled off his rain jacket and reversed it from the black exterior to the light gray inside lining, not caring how he looked to others.

The relief he felt at getting away faded as he realized that if he headed home, the Tundra men would just find him again. His insides felt like Jell-O and it took all his self-control not to vomit. The sick feeling got worse as the odors of the greasy food grew stronger. Jin pulled his hood low over his forehead and stepped outside. Now it was raining heavily. He didn't know where he was, but he knew he had to keep moving. He tried to read the street signs but he didn't recognize where he was. All he knew was that he was in southeast DC.

Suddenly, a black SUV pulled up right next to him. Jin panicked and wished he was in Mina's world. Immediately, he was pulled into sunshine and warmth as someone screamed and people gasped in shock.

Jin pushed off his hood and saw a woman pointing at him, yelling, "That boy appeared out of thin air!"

What looked like a tourist family, all wearing the same yellow T-shirt, gawked at him while other passersby seemed mystified.

"Did you see that? Did you see that?" the woman kept asking everyone around her.

Jin shoved past the bystanders and tore down the sidewalk. He needed to get as far away as he could before he jumped to his world. Worried that the Tundra men had recognized his rain jacket, he tore it off and let it drop to the ground. He was now in a black sweatshirt and jeans, and the warm weather was causing him to sweat. Seeing a tourist family meant that there had to be a hotel or a museum or other sightseeing location nearby. At the corner, he spotted a major intersection with lots of cars. It was Pennsylvania Ave and Third Street SE. He knew this area. By instinct he turned left. The gleaming white marble of the Library of Congress's John Adams Building was up ahead. Immediately heartened, Jin pushed himself harder. He made it to the corner where the two Library of Congress buildings faced each other before he was pulled back into a torrential downpour that soaked him to his core. Shivering, he ran to the ground-level entrance of the LOC's Thomas Jefferson Building and stood behind a group of tourists in rain ponchos waiting to go through security. Realizing he needed a pass to enter the library, Jin quickly scrolled the LOC website and saw there were plenty of same-day tickets available. He quickly reserved one with trembling fingers and a sigh of relief.

A middle-aged woman in front of him turned to look at him in shocked sympathy.

"Oh, you poor thing!" she said. Reaching into her bag under her large poncho, she pulled out a small packet. "Here, take this." She handed him a new poncho still in its packaging. "I bought too many and even though you're already soaked, you can dry off in the bathroom and use this going home."

Jin thanked her gratefully. He was happier about the ability to disguise himself from the men that were after him. Once past security, he darted over to the men's room to dry off as much as possible. His phone was beeping with texts from his friends asking where he was.

When he was relatively dry, Jin limped over to an empty bench behind the information desk and sat down. He had to think about what he wanted to do next. The Tundra men were probably waiting by his house for him to come home. He didn't want to bring danger to Meredith. It wasn't safe for him or her if he went home. What he needed was to be with more people. He was better off going to Mark's house.

Using his phone app, he requested a ride but saw that there was over a thirty-minute wait. Realizing it was due to the bad weather, Jin pulled up his phone map of the city. If he could get to Union Station, then he could catch a Red

Line train to a Metro stop that was about a fifteen-minute walk from Mark's house. But Jin was tired and in too much pain to move. He needed to rest. He decided to sit on the bench and close his eyes for just a moment . . . Jin woke up to a beam of sunlight shining in his face. Opening his eyes, he knew he'd jumped to Mina's world. He put a hand to his throbbing head. He felt even worse than before.

"Hey, kid, are you all right?"

A security guard came and stood right before him.

"Yeah, I'm fine," Jin replied. Trying not to stagger, he rose and headed for the stairs to the main floor. He didn't want to disappear in front of the guard and freak him out. He had no idea how long he'd been in this world. Once up in the beautiful Great Hall, Jin stood behind a column and glanced at his watch. He'd been asleep for about thirty minutes. He wondered if he'd been dreaming of Mina. But how long had he been here?

His question was answered when the bright light shining into the Great Hall dimmed as he felt his body pulled through space. The first thing he heard was the sound of hail pinging against the windows of the building.

Every single time he'd jumped worlds, the weather had gotten significantly worse. He had to stop teleporting and get somewhere safe.

Before going outside, he pulled on his new dark green poncho and sprinted into the storm. Tiny pieces of hail pelted him the entire way to the Metro station, but his poncho kept him from feeling the worst of it.

Forty-five minutes later, he was at Mark's house. As soon as his friends saw him, they burst out in laughter.

"Dude, what in the hell happened to you?" Liam asked.

"You look like all the reasons why I hate camping," Sam said.

"Jin, ignore them! Come in," Mark's mother said. "Let's get you some dry clothes while you take a shower."

Once safely inside, Jin felt the pain and exhaustion creep over him again. He was bone-tired, but he needed a shower desperately. In the bathroom, he saw why his friends had laughed. He was wet and covered in mud, leaves, grass, and dirt. Under the spray of the hot water, his whole body ached as if he'd been in a bad car accident. The back of his neck was sore and he could feel a burn scar forming from where the Taser had shocked him. He finally released all the fear he'd been holding back, and he shook violently. Dr. Vance was not just dangerous, he was evil. Jin had no choice—he had to tell his family what was happening.

When he went downstairs, the reaction was completely different from before. He had hidden his burn marks under the collar of the polo shirt Mark had lent him, but he couldn't hide the bruising spreading across his jaw.

"Dude! You look terrible, what happened?"

"I fell on my face," Jin replied, not willing to tell them what had really happened.

His friends started to laugh again, and Jin smiled, even though he felt like crying.

"Jin, you poor thing," Mark's mom said as she passed him an ice pack and some pills. "Take some ibuprofen and have some cookies and milk. It'll make you feel better."

After dinner, Mark drove him home with food for Meredith's dinner.

"Thanks for the ride," Jin said as he got out of the car.

Liam climbed over from the back to take the front seat. "Take it easy, Jin. Don't fall on your face again."

Sam and Mark laughed as they waved goodbye.

Once Jin was inside, Meredith popped out of her room to see him. "Jin, what happened to your face?" she asked in horror.

"I fell," Jin said shortly. "You hungry? Mark's mom sent home all this food to eat."

Immediately distracted by food, Meredith grabbed the bag and sat down at the kitchen table.

"Are you eating?" she asked as she opened up a container filled with pot roast and mashed potatoes.

"All yours," Jin called over his shoulder as he went up to his room.

Upstairs, Jin changed into his own clothes and crawled into bed. He began to shake, a belated reaction to all the stress of the day. Only then did he let the tears flow.

CHAPTER 24

Mina Is the Answer

Friday, May 16

Three days later, Jin woke up to the first quiet morning in days. No hurricane-force winds shaking the house. No ear-shattering thunder causing him to jump out of his skin. Best of all, there was no constant lashing and drumming of torrential rain against his window. It was a dark and cloudy day, but he was extremely relieved that it had stopped raining. The weather had been a colossal mess all over the world, and he knew it was because of how many times he had jumped between worlds the day he was tased. While the pain had subsided, the trauma would haunt him for many years to come. It was possibly the most frightening experience of his life.

Every night, he'd slept terribly. Waking up from a series of bad nightmares of being chased through the city. Of being tased and unable to breathe. But the one he'd had most recently was the worst. He'd been in Mina's world, holding her hand, when his body began to disappear. Inch by inch, he slowly vanished until he was completely gone and his consciousness sat in a void of nothingness. An incredible loneliness and deep grief erupted from his soul into a primal scream that rang in his head and woke him.

Today, he was determined to go to Mina's world and meet with Dr. Brennan and Dr. Prescott. He didn't want to live in fear of Tundra kidnapping him or of the threat to his very existence. He was tired of living with anxiety and dread. He just wanted it all to be over.

He put on a gray windbreaker and stepped out of his bedroom and froze. Through the sliding doors of the rooftop deck, he could see that the anomaly now stretched across the entire width of the sky. It had descended and grown as if it would swallow everything in its path. Jin's stomach roiled in nausea that surged into his throat. This was such a big change that it had to mean something monumental was going to happen soon.

He had to meet Mina right away. Whatever was going to happen between the two worlds was rapidly approaching. Jin knew he was running out of time.

Jin ran downstairs and was stopped by his father. His parents had arrived home with Jane last night. Jin was relieved they'd gotten home safe. Meanwhile Jane had barely said hello and gone straight to bed.

"Jin, good news, the police called and they caught the men who kidnapped you," Phil said. "They want you to come in today for a photo lineup. Let's go after you eat some breakfast."

"Uh, I can't now," Jin said. "I have to meet my friends."

"This is kind of important. Your friends can wait."

Jin thought for a moment about what would convince his dad to wait.

"Yeah, but this is really important also," he said. "There've been issues with the hotel possibly canceling prom and we're meeting to figure out what we can do to save it. I think morale would be destroyed if it was canceled."

This was all true, as he'd heard about it through Mark, since Diana and her friends were all on the prom committee. Mark had harassed Jin, Sam, and Liam about attending the meeting today. He just wasn't going.

"Oh my goodness, yes! That would be devastating," Alice responded. "You definitely need to go to that. Dad can take you to the police station later this afternoon, isn't that right, honey?"

Jin could see from his father's face that he would rather go straight to the police station, but he reluctantly agreed.

"Okay, I can give you a ride now and then come pick you up from school when you're done," Phil said. "What time will that be?"

Jin knew five hours was his max in Mina's world. It was now ten a.m.

"Around three," he replied. "But I don't need a ride. With road conditions being bad all over the city, it's probably faster to ride my bike." Jin knew he would need enough time to get back from the bookstore to school.

"That's too long, I need you to leave earlier, Jin. I'm sure they won't mind if I come get you by one p.m. at the latest," Phil said.

Jin opened his mouth to argue but could see that his dad was dead set on the time. Knowing he would have to leave and apologize for not being there later, Jin agreed.

Phil gave Jin a troubled look. "Be careful, son. Even though they caught the men, we don't know who else might be out there."

"I promise, I'll be perfectly safe," Jin said. "It's a nice day and people are out and about and I'll be in public or with others the whole time."

Waving goodbye to his parents, Jin left the house and rode down the block. From the corner of his eye, he saw another black SUV following him.

"Shit, they never stop," Jin said.

Determined to lose them, Jin took advantage of every alleyway he knew of, weaving in and out of alleys and streets until he came to the back of the local community center. He locked his bike to the rack and darted inside. The center was crowded with people taking advantage of the facilities. He saw several of his friends playing basketball and spotted Sam and Liam entering the lobby.

"Yo, Jin, you here to play some hoops?" Liam asked.

Jin shook his head as he eyed Liam's oversized black hoodie. "Do me a favor? Can you lend me your hoodie? And you can wear my jacket."

"Dude, I'll lend you my hoodie instead! That's a five-hundred-dollar Goose jacket!" Sam cut in.

Liam was already pulling his hoodie off. "No way! I got you. I tell you what, Jin, you can have all my hoodies for this jacket!"

Jin snorted. "I said lend, not have."

Snatching the jacket and shoving the hoodie into Jin's hands, Liam immediately put on the jacket and struck a pose. "How do I look?"

"Like a wannabe Jin," Sam responded.

"Piss off!"

Leaving them to their squabbles, Jin put on the hoodie and pulled the hood low over his face as he exited through the front of the community center. As he walked down the circular driveway, he saw the black SUV drive past him and into the parking lot. He grinned as he sauntered down the street and around the corner. Once he was out of view, he made a run for the bus stop. He managed to get on an extremely crowded bus that crawled through traffic even though it wasn't rush hour. Jin made it to the Book Nook just as it turned twelve. He was shocked to see that the shop was closed. All the stores on the block had a power outage.

"Crap!" He stood in front of the door and peered into the bookstore. How was he supposed to meet Mina if he wasn't inside the store? At that exact moment, he felt the buzzy rush and stomach-lurching motion of teleportation. The brightness of the sun hurt his eyes as someone yelled at him to get out of the way. He was standing in front of one of the doors to Wordplay. Inside, he could see Mina making her way to the back of the store.

"Mina!" he shouted in relief as he quickly entered Wordplay.

She turned around to see him enter and rush toward her.

"Jin, how are you outside?" Mina asked in shock, her voice muffled by his sudden embrace.

"Book Nook was closed in my world due to power outages," he said. "But since we were both thinking of each other, you pulled me here."

The thought resonated in his brain as important. *Mina*

is the reason I can come here. There was something more to it that he needed to figure out, but he filed the thought away for later.

Jin searched for a quiet, secluded corner away from the crowds. He grabbed two empty chairs and headed for a tiny alcove.

"I've been here every day this week hoping to see you." Mina sighed. "I'm so glad you came today!"

"It's been a hell of a week," Jin replied. He quickly filled her in on all that had happened in his world.

"We need Dr. Brennan and Dr. Prescott to help us," Mina said as she quickly texted them. "I can't believe the Tundra men tried to kidnap you."

She patted the faded bruises on his face lightly. "Does it still hurt?"

"Nah, I'm fine. And don't worry, they caught the men," Jin said, not mentioning the other car that was following him. "I think I'm safe for now."

Dr. Prescott responded immediately. She and Dr. Brennan were off campus but would head back soon. She asked them to meet at Dr. Brennan's office in two hours.

"We've got time," Mina said. "Should we go to the ramen place I told you about?"

Jin hesitated. Although he'd only been in Mina's world for a little while, he was already feeling weak. "I'm not really hungry and I think I would rather just stay here and talk with you."

Mina was immediately apprehensive. "Is there something wrong? Are you feeling all right?"

Not wanting her to worry more than she already was, Jin

shook his head. "I wanted to know what happened with your dad. Did he see my shoes?"

"Yeah, I told them they were Saachi's and she forgot them." Mina smirked. "She's got such huge feet he believed it."

"And did you eat fried chicken again?"

"Yes, I did, and I enjoyed it just as much the second time."

He laughed. Mina always made him feel happy when he was around her. When it was time to take the bus to George University, Jin stumbled as he got to his feet. The normal tiredness he felt in her world had worsened.

"Jin, your hand." Mina's voice was hushed, but he could still hear her panic.

His left hand looked translucent. Mina immediately pressed herself against his left side to hide it and ordered a ride.

"Quick, let's get out of here."

The car ride was quiet and tense. Mina's grip on Jin's arm was like a clamp, as if she was physically trying to keep him in her world. His left fingers had almost disappeared, but he could still feel them faintly. Mina hurried Jin over to the physics building, almost dragging him along as his weakness slowed him down.

The professors were shocked at Jin's appearance.

"The anomaly in my world has pretty much taken over the entire sky," Jin said. "And it looks like it's descending."

"It's starting," Dr. Prescott said. "Whatever is going to happen to your world has begun. Now the only thing Dr. Vance can do is try to imprison you in the underground lab."

"But how long does he have?"

"Only Jin could possibly know," Dr. Brennan responded. "Only Jin would be aware of what is happening."

"How do we save him?" Mina was in tears.

"We've looked and researched and tried to figure out a solution, but there's simply no scientific answer that can help you," Dr. Prescott said.

"Then what do we do?" Mina asked.

She was gripping Jin's hand so tightly it hurt. But it reminded him of the thought that had been forming in his brain. *Mina is the reason I can come here.*

What if there is no scientific answer and we're just wasting time looking for one? What if the answer is magic?

"It's Mina, the answer is Mina," Jin said.

"What are you saying?" Mina asked in confusion.

"Mina, I think you were right all along. We don't need science. We need magic and a miracle like the one you created in the first place," Jin said. "You caused the connection when you created the webcomic that bridged our two worlds. I think everything that's happened is because the bridge was never closed. You thought you closed it when you deleted the webcomic, but you said it yourself. It never got deleted!"

"I don't understand. You think everything that's happening is because the webcomic is continuing?" Mina asked.

"I think you need to finish the story."

Mina stared blankly at Jin. "What do you mean? How?"

"Write me into your world. Tell my story here. The one where I wake up completely cured and come home to my mom. My birth mom. And we get to grow up together and go to homecoming and prom." Jin's voice was husky with emotion. "You know. We get to have our fairy-tale ending."

Mina was shaking her head. "What kind of solution is this?"

"I think Jin's right," Dr. Prescott said. "I don't think physics is the answer. I think what we need is a miracle. And quickly, because you're running out of time."

The professor pointed to Jin's left forearm, which was now almost completely translucent.

"We are seeing something that doesn't make any sense in our real world, Mina," Dr. Prescott said. "By that logic, use the fantastical to find the solution."

"If I do this, what happens? How does it stop Jin from disappearing or jumping into another world?"

"I don't know," Dr. Prescott said. "But we have to try something."

"Mina, you created a story that changed my reality," Jin said. "I think you can do the same thing here now while my world is changing. Will you do it for me?"

"Of course, Jin. I'll do whatever it takes to save you."

"What is it you need?" Dr. Brennan asked. "I'm sure we can get it from the art department or even the library. But you have to start right away."

"It's okay, I have everything," Mina said. She pointed to her fanny pack. "I got in the habit of always carrying my mini drawing tablet with me everywhere."

"Will you be able to access your webcomic from here?" Dr. Prescott asked.

"Yes, but don't I need to make a new one?" Mina asked. "That webcomic created the whole mess."

"But that was also the starting point," Jin replied. "I think it needs to start and end there."

Mina was already booting up her drawing tablet. "So I should change the story to include you here?"

Thinking out loud, Jin said, "Mina, you don't have to do anything with what's already there. You could just add new chapters with backstory."

"Like a prequel? That will take too long. What about

how some webcomic artists like to do little biographies with short backstories on their characters? Would that work?" Mina asked, anxious to begin.

"Yes, definitely," Jin replied. *It has to.*

"Let's set you up in a conference room," Dr. Brennan said. "It'll be private and more comfortable than here."

Still holding hands, Jin and Mina followed Dr. Prescott and Dr. Brennan down the hall to a small corner conference room with floor-to-ceiling glass windows.

"I'll make sure no one bothers you in here," Dr. Brennan said. "Call me when you're done."

"Good luck," Dr. Prescott said as they both left the room.

"Do you think this will work?" Mina asked.

"It will," Jin replied. "I believe in you."

At his words, Mina shot him an anxious look. "I'm really nervous."

"Don't be, you've got this."

"And we have to do it now because you can't risk going back."

She sat down, pulling Jin into the seat next to her. "Luckily, I can draw pretty fast, especially when I don't have to color. I'll need both my hands. You're going to have to sit close and keep your hand on me. Whatever you do, don't let go!"

Aware of the danger waiting in his world if he blipped back, Jin nodded and placed his arm around her waist. He worried about his parents. He didn't want them to panic and think he'd been kidnapped. The thought of them immediately brought a more urgent issue to the forefront.

"Mina, you remember when my dad's accident was? Could you include a scene helping him get rid of the empty bird nest on the porch roof? If I'd been there, I would have done it for him and he wouldn't have fallen." Jin paused as he choked up at the thought of Phil's death in Mina's world.

Mina froze at his words. "Yes, I can do that."

She turned to look at him, and her eyes were glazed over with tears. "Jin, do you think I could have you and Auntie Jackie come to my house to stop my mom from driving the day of her accident?"

That day. The day Mina's life changed forever.

"Of course," Jin replied. "If we'd been there, she wouldn't have gone out."

Mina blinked away her tears, nodding before she took in a deep breath and began to draw.

Jin watched in amazement to see how talented Mina was. She quickly drew a chibi version of herself and Jin, with a detailed introduction. And then she began to create the backstory. The first part started with their moms being pregnant together, and it continued with baby Jin and Mina playing together, moving on to when they were riding tricycles. She captured their childhood in the space of a few panels. She then drew Jin lying on a hospital bed, his mom and Mina's mom sitting by his side.

In the caption, Mina wrote, *Jin got sick and had to go to the hospital. But he had a complete and full recovery and was able to go home that same day*.

The next panel showed little Jin and Mina holding hands and exiting the hospital doors with their mothers behind them.

At that moment, a wave of dizziness overcame Jin. He looked down. His left leg was now translucent. Not wanting to freak Mina out, he didn't say anything. But he felt terribly weak. Even keeping his arm around Mina's waist took effort. Gently, he rested his head on her shoulder.

She was now drawing Jin as a young teenager, looking a little more sullen next to a chipper Mina, who was poking her finger into his dimple.

"Jin, what are some of your favorite things to do?" she asked as she continued to rapidly draw.

"Soccer, basketball, tennis, watching you eat," he answered softly.

Mina laughed as she immediately launched into a panel of Jin playing all three sports. In each one, a cheering Mina could be seen in the crowd. The last sketch was of Jin watching Mina stuff her mouth full of his favorite jajangmyeon noodles.

Jin looked down at himself again and realized he could no longer see the left side of his body and his right leg had turned translucent.

"Mina, don't look, but I think you have to hurry," he whispered.

"I'm drawing as fast as I can," she said.

He could see her hand tremble, and he gave her a reassuring squeeze with the little strength he still had.

She drew high school Jin with scenes from classrooms to homecoming to college acceptance day. She added Jin on a ladder clearing out a bird's nest and then Jin and Auntie Jackie coming to her house, both with dates written on each panel.

Jin released the breath he had been holding. He hoped that was enough to change several lives.

"Quick, call the professors and ask them to come here!"

"I don't think I can, Mina," Jin replied softly.

This time Mina turned to look fully at Jin. "Oh my god, no, Jin!" Mina grabbed her phone and called Dr. Brennan and begged him to come right away. They heard him and Dr. Prescott running down the hall before they both entered the room.

"Professor, he's disappearing! What do I do?"

Dr. Brennan and Dr. Prescott looked at each other.

"I think it's time to let him go, Mina," Dr. Prescott said.

"No, he'll be in danger!"

"If he stays any longer, he will disappear forever. Let him go, and finish the webcomic and load it ASAP. It's the only way to save him."

"Jin," Dr. Brennan said, "if Dr. Vance knows you are on campus, and I'm positive he's been tracking you, he will have Tundra Labs' private security capture you. Do whatever you have to do to get campus police to protect or arrest you instead. Dr. Vance's plan is to imprison you in one of Tundra Labs' underground vaults to keep you from teleporting. You must not be taken to TULLY. Remember that."

Mina was crying. "Jin, I love you. I'm almost done, I'll see you again. Remember, don't let them lock you away!"

"I love you, Mina," Jin said. He let go just as he lost sensation in the arm that was holding on to her.

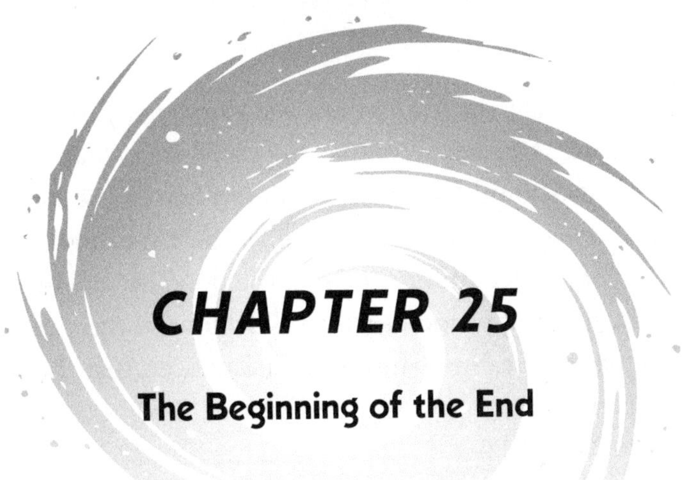

CHAPTER 25

The Beginning of the End

Jin felt the immediate buzzing and lurching stomach of the transfer. He had closed his eyes because of how weak he'd felt. But now he felt fine. He opened his eyes to see he was in the same conference room without Mina. Running his hands over himself, he realized he was completely solid again. He stepped over to the windows and froze in shock. The entirety of the skies had been taken over by the massive, swirling abyss. It had descended almost to the tops of the highest buildings. Jin knew he had to get out of the building. But Dr. Brennan had seemed sure Dr. Vance was tracking him, even though Jin no longer had the thumb drive. Yet it made sense. Jin had weaved through a lot of different alleyways, but the Tundra men still were able to follow him. He'd lost them after he switched his jacket for Liam's sweatshirt.

His phone! He'd left it in the pocket of his jacket. That was how they'd been able to track him down. But now they were following Liam. Jin smirked and wondered if they would even realize that they were tracking the wrong Asian.

So they should have no idea he was here. However, just in case, he should let his father know. There was no landline in the conference room. Opening the door, he saw that the hallway was empty and quietly walked toward the elevators. As he passed Dr. Brennan's office, he noticed that the door was open.

"Dr. Brennan?"

Jin entered the room, but the office was empty. Guilt stopped him in his tracks. Where was this world's Dr. Brennan? Jin could only pray that he was safe somewhere. Spotting a landline on the professor's desk, he went over and called his dad's cell phone. The call went right to voicemail.

"Dad! I'm sorry I didn't tell you what I was doing, but I'm at George University's Department of Physics and I think the men that tried to kidnap me work for Tundra Labs. I don't have my phone, but can you come and get me? I'll be waiting out front in fifteen minutes."

Jin sat at the table where he'd first met with Dr. Brennan. On the whiteboard, he could still see part of the notes on their conversation, where the professor had drawn little Jin figures in different worlds. Across the middle of the whiteboard, in large letters, he spotted the professor's messy scrawl.

Find the place that exists in the space between.

He had no idea what it meant, but he was sure it was a message for him. He didn't understand why the professor would leave it here in his office. It grieved him to think that Dr. Brennan might be hurt or imprisoned or worse. Jin could only hope that when the worlds merged, the Dr. Brennan here would safely merge with the one in Mina's world. And that whatever hardships he was dealing with now would be completely forgotten.

Jin glanced at his watch. Ten minutes had passed. He should go and wait for his father. As he was about to leave, he spotted a navy-blue George baseball cap. Swiping it, he pulled it low over his forehead and took the elevator down.

In the lobby, Jin walked swiftly past the security guard desk and the lounge area.

"Hey, this building is closed to students! How'd you get in here?" a campus security guard yelled at him.

"I was here already, working up in the physics lab all day," Jin lied. "I didn't see you when I came in."

"Nobody is supposed to be in here," the guard continued. "Who let you in? It's not safe. Didn't you see the notices?"

The guard pointed at paper taped up at the front entrance. At that moment, uniformed guards appeared in front of the doors. Jin's flight instinct took over and he ran toward another exit, but more men came into the building. He was now surrounded by security wearing jackets with Tundra logos on them. The Tundra guards pointed their Tasers and screamed at him to get on the floor.

Jin glanced at the campus security guard.

"Call the police!" Jin yelled. "They're trying to kidnap me! They have guns!"

The guard immediately picked up his walkie-talkie and shouted "Emergency!" as he rushed outside.

The Tundra guards manhandled Jin onto his stomach.

They held him face-down on the ground as Jin heard footsteps approaching him.

"Jin, you really have a lot of explaining to do," Dr. Vance said, kneeling down in front of his face. "You've been lying to me. Not telling me of your little excursions. Spending longer and longer away from your real world. I was almost beginning to worry. But I'm glad you're back. We're finally going on that ride I've been telling you about. Don't worry. We will take good care of you."

"How'd you find me?" Jin asked.

"Ah, you mean after you left your phone with your friend?" Dr. Vance asked. "It's because you came back here. Anywhere else and it would have been difficult. But we have cameras all over this building. I got an alert as soon as you poofed into the conference room."

"You're insane! Why are you doing this to me?" Jin yelled.

"You are the human embodiment of what we've only discovered at the quantum level," Dr. Vance said. "We've long believed that nothing more than information could be teleported between two particles. But here you are. Teleporting through worlds like a bouncing Ping-Pong ball when science says it is not only impossible, but it should theoretically have killed you. We need to study this miracle."

"I'm not a lab rat, I'm a human. You can't lock me away!"

"We have no choice! While you are a science marvel, you are also endangering this entire planet with your actions. It has always been easy to sacrifice the liberties of one if it is for the greater good."

"You mean your satellite project! This is all about money and your ambition!"

Dr. Vance smiled. "What a smart boy you are! As a matter

of fact, you are absolutely right. Your ping-ponging across the universe has cost me millions in delays. We're bleeding money because of you. And you're going to make it up to us."

Dr. Vance stood up. "Take him to TULLY."

The Tundra guards dragged Jin out of the building to where large black SUVs were waiting. Before they could reach the vehicles, several police cars drove up and blocked them. Officers with drawn weapons poured out of the cars, shouting orders. From the back of one of the squad cars, Jin saw his father get out.

"That's my son!" he yelled.

"Police! Drop your weapons! Put your hands behind your heads!"

The Tundra guards did not immediately comply. Instead, they drew their guns and closed ranks around Jin. Dr. Vance stepped forward to speak with the police.

"Officers, there's been a terrible mistake. I'm a professor here at the university. But I am also with Tundra Labs, working with the military on a highly classified project. We must take this research subject back to the lab. He is a danger to public safety."

"He's lying! They're kidnapping me! I'm not even a student here!" Jin shouted.

"I assure you that is not what is happening," Dr. Vance said in a placating manner. "He has been exposed to extreme levels of radiation. If we were to allow you to take him, then you would also be exposed and have to quarantine. We have no choice but to isolate him for everyone's sake—"

"No one is going anywhere!" The lead police officer cut the professor off.

"This is a matter of national security!" Dr. Vance shouted. "You do not have authority here. We have the highest military clearance for our program. And I'm afraid I cannot let you take this subject."

The Tundra guards blocked the police in a standoff. Dr. Vance pulled Jin back toward the building, but Jin resisted.

"I'm not going with you," he said.

"If you don't, then you are risking the safety of your family and everyone around you," Dr. Vance responded fiercely.

"You're a liar," Jin replied just as fiercely. "You want to lock me up at TULLY in an underground vault. You want to experiment on me like a lab animal."

"Damn it, Jin! You are going to be responsible for the destruction of this entire world! I am trying to save us! Save our world!" Dr. Vance was shouting.

"The other Dr. Brennan says you can't stop what is inevitable."

Dr. Vance laughed. "Easy to say when his world is not the one in peril. Who's to say something even greater can't come out of this world if we save it!"

"The something greater being your billion-dollar satellite project? That's just money!"

Jin could see that the police officers had edged closer, still circling them.

"Drop the weapon!" an officer with a bullhorn shouted.

Dr. Vance pulled Jin closer. "We have to go now."

Jin planted his feet, refusing to move. "I'm not going with you. And you can't make me."

"That's where you're wrong," Dr. Vance replied. "Mason, Petrov, take him inside."

Two of the Tundra guards twisted Jin's arms behind his back and dragged him toward the building.

"Release him!" the officer with the bullhorn yelled as other officers moved closer.

One of the Tundra men pointed his gun at Jin's head. Over the man's shoulder, Jin locked eyes with his father. He could see the fear and horror on his face. This was not what Jin wanted for his dad. As it was, he was afraid of what might happen when their worlds collided—the very strong possibility that if Mina wasn't successful, there wouldn't be a Jin or a Phil in her world. Jin desperately prayed that he would see Mina again.

Immediately, his body jerked out of the grip of the Tundra men and he had the sensation of free-falling before he landed hard on his hands and knees in front of the physics building.

"Holy shit!" someone shouted. "Did that guy just fall out of the sky?"

A student in a red cap came over and extended a hand to help Jin up.

"I saw you poof into existence!" he said excitedly. "How the hell did you do that?"

The other students were now gathered around him.

"Was that some sort of magic trick?"

"I swear he just appeared out of nowhere!"

Jin ignored all of them. He was still discombobulated from the jump.

He looked at his watch. Twenty seconds had passed. He looked around the front of the building and decided to hide behind one of the large columns. That way he would still be close to the action but out of the Tundra guards' reach. The red-capped student who insisted he'd seen him magically appear kept following him and asking questions. Jin was too worried about his situation to pay any attention to the annoying student. As he stood behind the column facing the building's door, he couldn't help but think how close Mina was.

When the jump happened, he caught sight of the annoying student's shocked excitement as he vanished. Jin reappeared in his world to shouting and confusion. He peeked out at the square and saw that the Tundra guards had surrendered their arms and were being arrested by the police. Dr. Vance stood calmly in front of the police, but his eyes were scanning the area, looking for Jin.

"Where's Jin? Where's my son?"

Jin heard his father frantically shouting for him.

"Dad!" Jin stepped out from behind the column and slowly walked toward his father.

"There he is." Dr. Vance smiled. "Now do you believe me? He is a danger to our world."

Nobody was listening to him. A police officer came over to Jin and asked if he was all right and led him toward his father.

Dr. Vance screamed as they handcuffed him.

"Jin, you are responsible for the destruction of the entire planet! Everyone will die because of you! How will you live with yourself?"

"Hey, don't listen to that weirdo, kid, he doesn't make any sense," the policeman said. "You'll be okay now. Here's your dad."

Phil pulled Jin into a tight embrace.

"Officer, can I take my son home now?" he asked. He was clearly still deeply shaken up.

"Yeah, sure," the officer responded. "You'll need to file a police report, but we can do all that at your house. Let's get you both home."

As Jin got into the car, he could see the swirling abyss descending closer. He looked up to see the top of a building disappear before his eyes.

Phil sat in the back of the cruiser with Jin, keeping an arm tight around his shoulders. Jin leaned against him and relaxed. While the police officer chatted with his father, Jin closed his eyes and tried to rest.

When they pulled up in front of their house, Alice came bursting through the door and hugged Jin. He had to smile as she yelled at him. With the fate of the world hanging over his head, he was relieved to see her one last time.

"There was a kidnapping attempt on your son," the police officer said.

"Again? Did you catch them? Is he safe now?"

"Yes, we caught the suspects."

"Oh, thank god!" Alice cried. "Jin, you must have been terrified!"

Jin wasn't paying attention. He was staring up at the sky. The abyss was hanging below the treeline. Everything it touched had vanished.

"Look at the sky," Jin said, wondering if anyone else could see what he was seeing.

They all looked. Alice sighed. "Looks like another bad storm," she said. "Let's all go inside."

It was destroying their world, and yet no one could see it but him.

Just then, the squawking of the policeman's radio pierced the air with an urgent command. The officer responded immediately and ran back to his patrol car, apologizing and asking them to bring Jin to the station for an interview.

Jin hardly noticed what was happening. He saw something that made him hopeful. Deep within the churning abyss, he spotted something he'd never seen before: a small area where the blackness of space was fading into blue skies again. The worlds were merging. He could see it clearly. He knew instinctively that it was Mina's world he was seeing. He wasn't sure why this was a good sign, but it felt like a lifeline had been thrown his way. In his heart, he knew that Mina had been successful. Now he had to figure out what he had to do.

Find the place that exists in the space between.

Dr. Brennan had written that on the whiteboard in his office for Jin to see. But what had he meant? Suddenly, everything crystalized.

"The portal!"

The bookstore had always been the one place Jin could exist between both worlds. That was the space between! A sudden gut feeling told him he had to go there immediately. Before the anomaly took over the entirety of his world.

He turned to face his adoptive parents. They were looking at him with concern.

"Jin, are you okay? Were you hurt? We can worry about going to the police station later. Should we go to the hospital?" Phil asked.

Jin felt a rush of love toward the two people who had helped him when he needed it most. Despite the trauma and hardship he'd endured, they'd never made him feel unloved or unwanted. For that, he was truly grateful. He knew that if his and Mina's plan worked and he was able to transition to

Mina's world, his relationship with them would never be the same. This moment was bittersweet, but he leaned into his sadness over having to say goodbye.

He choked back his tears and hugged Phil and then Alice.

"I just want you to know that I love you both a lot," he said. "Thank you for being there for me. Thank you for raising me. I'll never forget you. But I have to go now."

Before they could react, Jin looked for his bicycle and remembered he'd left it at the community center. He saw Jane's mint-green bicycle lying haphazardly on the porch. Jumping onto his sister's bike, Jin raced off. He could hear them calling after him, asking where he was going.

He knew where he needed to go. He just hoped he could reach it in time. As he biked down the street, he saw Meredith and Jane walking home together.

"Jin! There you are! We've been worried sick over you!" Meredith shouted.

"Sorry, Merry! Hi, Jane! I have to go!"

"Where are you going with my bike?" Jane yelled.

"Love you both!"

They chased after him. But he didn't stop. He kept pedaling until he hit the main road.

Where the abyss was touching the tall buildings, he could see them disappearing and reappearing above it.

This was it. He still didn't know what would happen to him, but he knew he had to get to the bookstore. As he biked, new things were happening. A Metrobus drove past him and suddenly the rumble of its engine went silent. He turned his head and saw that the bus was gone. This brought him to a halt, and he looked behind him. The area he had come from was covered in a thick gray mist. People on the sidewalks and cars on the street heading into the mist disappeared. Swallowed by heavy gray clouds that were creeping closer to him.

Jin was trying not to panic—he just rode ahead as fast as he could pedal. He was still a mile away, but the changes were happening all around him. In the blue sky above the abyss, he could see a plane. He realized that it must be from Mina's world. It was as if he was half in and half out of her world, just like when he was in the bookstore.

The space between.

Up ahead, he could hear the sounds of people out and about in the shopping center as usual. But above them, the gray clouds were descending rapidly. He reached the center just as the abyss swallowed the entire area. One by one, the people around him disappeared into the mist. He was in a heavy fog that was absolutely silent. He couldn't hear anyone anymore. He was all alone.

This is what the end of the world looks like, Jin thought.

People vanishing right in front of his eyes. Buildings disappearing. The gray fog blotted out the sky and surrounded him. He dropped his bike and kept walking as quickly as he could, staring only at the cracks of the sidewalk at his feet. Reaching out an arm, he felt a building next to him. It was a doorway. He peered through the window and realized it was Bread & Butter. He was close. He kept a finger grazing the stone walls of the buildings as he counted two more storefronts before he was finally at the Book Nook. Lights were on, but the door was locked. He threw himself against the door, but it didn't budge. In desperation, he grabbed a heavy iron chair from the sidewalk and flung it through the storefront window. The shattering of the glass was strangely muted. The store was eerily quiet and empty.

Jin climbed into the front of the store and fell over the chair and a book display. He landed hard in a pile of shattered glass. He could feel the shards slicing into his hand and knee. Cursing in pain, he stood up unsteadily and limped as fast as he could toward the back room.

Behind him, the gray fog seeped into the store close on his heels. The portal door to Mina's world was only steps away. He could see the bright fluorescent lights and people moving about. Excited by the safety that he could see through the window, Jin tripped and fell over a pile of books strewn across the floor. When he tried to rise, he saw that his legs were translucent. He could barely feel them. He tried to rise, but something was sapping him of his strength. The sensation was similar to the one he'd had in the conference room. Extreme fatigue and the terrible sense that he was losing himself. He could no longer feel his legs, and there was a growing numbness in his arms. He dropped his head into his arms and thought of Mina.

I think we were too late, Mina. Tell my mom I love her.

He closed his eyes.

No, Jin, get up!

He heard Mina's voice in his head.

Hurry up! You can do this!

Mina. She was waiting for him.

He had to reach the portal door. He looked at his legs. They were faded but still there. He could still see the blood dripping from his knee.

Gathering all his strength, Jin crawled forward and got

onto his feet, stumbling as he navigated the book stacks. He focused on the bright light ahead. It was the portal door. Wordplay was right there. With the last of his strength, Jin reached for the door and pushed himself through.

He had made it.

CHAPTER 26

Home at Last

He burst through the portal door and his exhaustion and weakness disappeared. He was safe in Mina's world.

Overwhelming relief made him giddy, and he steadied himself on a bookshelf. He noticed that his hand was fine. The cuts from the broken glass had vanished. Even his knee was healed. No trace of any blood remained on his clothing or body. He gazed through the portal window to see if he could still see the Book Nook, but now it was nothing but a storage room.

The portal to his world was gone.

He walked slowly, avoiding browsing customers, as he headed toward the front of the store where the exits were. Would he be able to leave on his own? Hesitating, he moved forward and pushed open the door. In the next moment, he was outside. Shading his eyes from the bright sunlight, he looked around, and for a moment, it was as if his vision had split into two different screens. One of his previous world and the other of the new one he'd just stepped into. Both were completely familiar to him. The memory of the Book Nook was still clear. He could still recall the different stores that made up the shopping mall around it. But it was as if the two memories were blending into one another. There had been a makeup store, but now it was across the street. The Bread & Butter café was in both worlds, but it was bigger here. Or was it? As the two memories merged, he became a little confused. His brain was a confusing patchwork of conflicting realities. He had to try to keep them apart. He needed to remember that this was now Mina's world.

Mina!

He needed to see her. He pushed past the confusing memories and focused solely on finding Mina. He had to tell her that it had worked. A heady rush of euphoria sent a surge of heat through his body. He really was here. She'd done the impossible and saved him. Wandering around the shopping center, he thought she had to be near. That was the only way he could have come to her world.

No, wait. That was before, Jin thought to himself. *Everything has changed now.*

Jin walked to the bus stop as the bus pulled in. He jumped on without thinking, pulled out his wallet, and used his Metro card to pay the fare. Only when he sat down did he stare at the Metro card in surprise. It had worked in Mina's world. Which meant it was from here. He opened his wallet and pulled out his student ID. It said *Jin Young* instead of *Jin Young Kanter*.

He was no longer a Kanter. So many mixed emotions swirled inside him, but the sharpest was the grief that caused his breath to hitch and his heart to painfully contract. It eased as he was flooded with visions of two different experiences, both happy and sorrowful.

Two different lived experiences were warring inside his head. One told him he should be surprised at all these new changes, while the other one reassured him that he'd lived another life right here. He was staring out the window when the bus passed a familiar intersection. Impulsively, he pressed the request next stop button. When he alighted from the bus, his feet took him to the intersection. It looked the same in both worlds. He turned left and walked down several familiar blocks. He'd walked them thousands of times before. On the corner, he spotted a house he knew well. The Kanter house. Looking all the way up at the fourth floor, Jin could remember standing on the rooftop terrace. He could see parents and two sisters with him at mealtimes. The warmth and laughter of family.

Suddenly, the door opened and out stepped Phil Kanter with a large goldendoodle on a leash. The dog bounded over to say hi to Jin.

"Well, hello there," Phil said with a smile, the excited dog wagging its tail enthusiastically by his side. "You're the young man who helped me years ago with that bird nest! How have you been?"

Jin blinked back his tears of relief. Mina had saved Dr. Kanter also. All was good.

"Hi, Da . . . Dr. Kanter, it's really great to see you."

Phil shook Jin's hand as the excited dog rubbed himself against Jin's legs.

"So, are you in college now?" Phil asked.

"No, I just graduated, I'm going to Johns Hopkins," Jin replied. He marveled that this detail had stayed the same.

"Oh, that's wonderful! We just came back from bringing our oldest home from Oberlin. College is a fun time. Good luck!" Phil smiled warmly at him.

As Jin raised his hand in goodbye, Phil caught sight of Jin's watch.

"Hey, that's a Seiko Speedtimer! I used to have one just like it," he said approvingly. "You have excellent taste in watches, son."

"Thanks," Jin said, his voice raspy with emotion. "It's very special to me."

He watched Dr. Kanter walk away with his dog. Two memory threads were now intertwined in his mind. Both were real, but the one he was in right now was his new reality.

The sadness he'd felt earlier at losing the Kanter name returned in full force. Having gained back the world he'd lost, he would now have to say goodbye to those who were familiar to him. Who he had called family. Jin was feeling a mix of emotions. Love and anger, gratitude and resentment, it was all churning in his head. But in his heart, the pain of saying goodbye was first and foremost.

He stood for a long moment watching as Dr. Kanter and his dog grew smaller, until they turned a corner and he could no longer track them. Only then did he proceed to where his heart told him he had to go. Retracing his steps to the familiar intersection, but this time going straight. A right turn, then left. His seething emotions had calmed. There was a serene happiness growing within him that replaced his confusion and grief. As he approached Mina's house, he could feel his excitement. When the door opened and Mina stepped out into the walkway, his heart tightened in a wildly painful joy. He almost couldn't believe his eyes. She looked different and yet wonderfully familiar. Her dark hair still framed the same beautiful heart-shaped face, but it was longer and without the gray ombre. And the slight air of melancholy that had always seemed a part of her was gone. Instead, she exuded a happy contentment that brightened her eyes and warmed her smile. She was the same Mina and yet fundamentally changed.

"Jin, where have you been? Did you forget your phone again?"

Breaking into a run, he scooped her up.

"Are you okay?" Mina asked. "Did something happen?"

"You did it! You saved me!" Jin twirled her around in his arms.

"Yay! I'm glad! But what are you talking about?" Mina laughed.

"Your webcomic! It worked. It brought me here!"

She furrowed her eyebrows in confusion. "My webcomic? But I haven't even released the first episode yet. What do you mean it worked?"

Jin's eyes widened in shock. He'd just assumed that after all they'd been through, Mina would remember it all. Despite everything, she would be his constant. But in the process of changing Jin's story, Mina's memory had been affected.

"I meant the idea of it was exciting, it brought me here to see you," Jin said, prevaricating.

She eyed him suspiciously. "You're excited by a romance?"

"Who doesn't love a good love story?" Jin grinned.

"Huh, well, I'm still trying to figure out the setting," Mina continued. "I was thinking of setting it in our high school—"

"Definitely not there!" Jin cut in, thinking of her previous webcomic with a shudder. "I mean, we're graduating. You should set it on a college campus instead. I have an idea! We can go to George's campus so you can take reference photos, and I'll bring a picnic."

Mina nodded thoughtfully. "Yes, I like that idea. Especially the picnic part!"

Jin hugged her again and was leaning in for a kiss when Mina put her whole hand in his face.

"Jin! You're in front of my house! Behave!"

Jin pouted.

"Come in already," Mina said opening the front door. "My mom wanted me to bring a bunch of cucumbers and peppers over to your house. But now we can go together."

Jin stared in surprise. "Your mom?"

"Yeah, you know how she has that little vegetable patch out back? You will now be forced to eat fresh vegetables all summer long."

"Mom, Jin's here!" Mina yelled.

In total shock, Jin watched as Mina's mom appeared from the kitchen holding a brown shopping bag. She was both familiar and new. But as she approached, the newness faded away into a familiar love.

"Aunt Emma," Jin said as he gave her a hug.

"Jin," she said warmly. "Either you're getting taller or I'm shrinking!"

"You say that all the time," Jin responded. And he realized this was a conversation he'd had with her many times. Where were these memories coming from?

"Your mom's been calling this past hour trying to find you," Mina's mom went on. "You left your phone at home."

Mom. Jin's heart thudded. "I'd better get home right away then," he said.

"I'll go with you," Mina said. "But you hold the bag. It's heavy."

Stepping outside, Jin froze as he tried to figure out which way to go.

"What are you doing?" Mina asked as she walked past him. "You forgot the way home or something?"

She slid her hand into his and pulled him along. "You okay, Jin? You're acting a little off today."

"I'm fine," he said. "Did you get your dress for prom yet?"

"Your mom is still working on it," Mina said. "I can't wait to see it!"

"Me too."

"Auntie Jackie is the best," Mina continued. "I can't believe she made the time for me when she's literally the wedding dress designer of the rich and famous!"

"Doesn't matter, you're her most important client," Jin stated.

"You sound just like her." Mina giggled.

"I wonder what color it is."

"You haven't peeked yet?"

Jin shook his head.

"Well, don't! Promise me you won't. I want you to be blown away when you see me," Mina said.

"It doesn't take much to do that," Jin replied sincerely.

Mina stopped and stood on tiptoe to place her hands on either side of Jin's face. "Are you sure you're okay? Is this really my Jin Young?"

Jin leaned forward to kiss her. "Always and forever yours."

"That was kind of cringy," she laughed.

"You still love me," he replied. Even as confused as he was, his heart was overflowing with happiness. This world was his.

Jin held Mina's hand as they walked the last few blocks to the place he'd been aching for his whole life. The way was a dear memory from long ago, when he was little and innocent. He'd taken this path with his mom many times over. He knew which of the town houses was his as soon as he saw it. This was the home of his dreams. It was the only one with a beautiful teal-blue door and an elegant flower wreath. As they approached, the door opened and a little white dog came waddling out. His stubby tail wagged elatedly.

"Mochi! Come here, boy!" Mina bent down to say hello to Mochi, but he ran right around her to jump on Jin.

"Wow, what's up with him? He's acting like he hasn't seen you in a while!"

Jin dropped his bag to pick up the gleefully wriggling dog, who promptly tried to lick every inch of his face.

"Mochi, stop trying to clean his face like that!" Jin's mother stepped out with a huge smile.

His mother. She looked beautiful and vibrant as he'd always remembered her. He'd missed her so much. But in his other memory, he had seen her this morning. Both were true, and it filled him with a happiness that the Jin from the other world had never experienced.

"Jin, Mina, just in time for dinner!" she said.

"Mom," Jin choked. He passed Mochi to Mina and rushed to hug his mother. She was warm and smelled like honeysuckle and laundry soap.

"Oh, honey, are you okay?" Jackie asked. "I was going to

yell at you about forgetting your phone again. You know how I worry when I can't get ahold of you."

She gently pushed Jin into the house and handed him a cell phone, which Jin put in his pocket. "I promise I won't forget it again," he said, wiping the tears from his eyes.

Inside, the house was exactly as he remembered it. Pretty pastel walls, oversized sofas and armchairs, and flower arrangements everywhere. The interior showcased his mother's personality perfectly. He took it all in with the biggest smile.

"Did something happen? Are you all right?" she asked in concern.

"I'm fine." Jin kept smiling. "I'm better than fine. I'm great."

Mina brought Mochi and the bag of vegetables into the house and gave Jin's mother a hug. Mochi immediately went over to try to jump on Jin again.

"Hi, Aunt Jackie! Jin is acting really weird."

"I'm not weird," he laughed. "I'm just really appreciating the people in my life."

Mina blinked her eyes and asked, "Okay, who are you and what did you do to my best friend?"

At that exact moment, Jin saw a flurry of visions of Mina when he'd first seen her through the webcomic. They were followed by memories of the new timeline. Hanging at her house, dinner with both their families, studying at the library, amusement park trips, and parties and so much more. These visions now formed the basis for his new reality.

"Listen, I was imagining a life where I was separated from both of you and it was just horrifying. And I realized I would do anything I could to get back to you and Mom," he said. "I couldn't survive without you both."

"Well, I couldn't imagine a life without the two of you either, and I don't want to!" his mother exclaimed. She patted his cheek softly and smiled. "Luckily we don't have to."

Jin hugged her again. "I love you, Mom."

"Love you too," she said. "Mina, stay for dinner. I'll call your mom. That way she can have a date night with your dad."

"Okay, Aunt Jackie," Mina said.

Jackie went into the kitchen with Mochi following at her heels. Jin stood blinking back the tears that welled in his eyes again. He wondered if it was okay for him to feel this happy.

Tilting her head like a curious puppy, Mina got on her tiptoes and gave Jin a loud smooch.

Still caught up in his emotions, Jin looked at her in surprise.

"What was that for?" he asked.

"You looked like you needed it."

I needed you and you saved me, he thought. She didn't realize what she'd done. But he could never forget. *Mina, I love you.*

Caressing her face, Jin bent down and kissed her. It was the sweetest of kisses that conveyed all his love and melted away the remaining slivers of loneliness in his heart.

"What was that for?" she asked.

"I really needed it," he responded.

"You feel better now?"

Jin hugged her tight.

"Never better," he sighed. And he meant it.

AWARDS AND ACKNOWLEDGMENTS

Best Editor Extraordinaire—Phoebe Yeh

Best Brilliant Agent—Marietta Zacker

Best Awesome Editorial Assistant—Daniela Cortes

Best Hair in Publishing and President—Mallory Loehr

Best and Most Talented Art Team—Angela Carlino and Michelle Gengaro-Kokmen

Best Fabulous Cover Artist—Robin Har

Best and Smartest Copyediting/Managing Editorial Team—Alison Kolani, Patricia Callahan, Jamie Johnson, Barbara Perris, Rebecca Vitkus, Kiffin Steurer, and Harshdeep Kaur

Best and Funnest School and Library Team—Adrienne Waintraub, Katie Halata, Erica Trotta, Michelle Campbell, and Natalie Capogrossi

Best Writer Crew Who Absolutely Rocks—Axie Oh, Kat Cho, Meredith Buse, and Hena Khan

Best Family and Support Team (who also drives me crazy, but I love you all so much)—Sonny, Summer, Skye, and Graysin Oh

Best and Cutest and Sweetest Pup—Kiko

Best Grumpy Pup Who Bites—Tokki

Don't miss out on the beginning of Jin and Mina's love story!

When Mina, a Korean American teenage artist, gets sucked into the world of her own web comic, she must find a way out with the help of a cute boy, all while facing off against a villainous corporation.

CHAPTER 1

First Day of Senior Year

Monday, August 29, Washington, DC

Mina stood under her umbrella in the pouring rain, staring with dread at the doors of Bellington High School, a big imposing redbrick building that loomed above her like every scary mansion in the horror movies she despised watching.

First day of senior year.

First day of hell.

"Mina Lee, get your butt inside before we drown to death!" Her best friend, Saachi, grabbed Mina by the arm and began pulling her up the stairs.

Mina heaved a great big sigh as they joined the mass of students filing into the school through the imposing entranceway. The girl in front of her whipped back curly wet hair, slapping Mina across her face.

Mina flinched and swatted the hair away, causing the girl to turn and glare at her.

"Do you mind?"

Mina narrowed her eyes, her nostrils flaring with displeasure. "Yes, I do mind. I don't like eating hair for breakfast."

The girl turned without another word.

"Did you say something?" Saachi asked.

Before Mina could respond, an elbow rammed into her lower spine.

She whimpered. "I am a sardine packed tight into a smelly tin can of death."

"What are you mumbling to yourself?" Saachi asked. At five foot ten, Saachi could use her height to maneuver deftly through the crowds without getting hurt.

"I am a bunny rabbit caught in the coils of a deadly python."

"I am a girl who doesn't want to be late to her first class," Saachi cut in. Apparently annoyed at the snail's pace, she barged ahead, scattering kids left and right as she shouted "Excuse me!" at the top of her lungs.

"I am a salmon swimming against the current into the gaping jaws of death," Mina intoned. They'd finally made it inside the expansive lobby that led to hallways spiderwebbing into the depths of the building.

"Listen, can you save your existential crisis for exams?"

Mina stopped in her tracks, causing Saachi to nearly trip and fall. "What's the point, Saachi?"

"Mina," Saachi said threateningly.

Students yelled their frustration at Mina, some even shoving her. But Mina refused to budge. She might be only five three, but she was a mighty five three and could plant her feet like small sledgehammers.

"I mean why am I even here? What's the point when I don't know what the future entails? My dad thinks he has my life all figured out, but I don't want what he wants. Do I? I mean what am I supposed to do? What do I need to do? Do I just listen to my father like a good Asian daughter?"

"Girl, I will pick you up and haul you into first period. I am not playing," Saachi fumed.

Mina saw the murderous intent in her friend's eyes and released a heavy sigh. "All right." She shuffled her feet to move forward, letting Saachi drag her. "I am a pawn in someone else's chess game of life."

"Shut up, Mina! Where's your first class?"

Mina pulled out her schedule and peered down at it morosely.

First period, Psychology, Salatto, Rm 246
Second period, Honors Calculus, Khan, Rm 225
Third period, AP Studio Art, Ellis, Rm G84
Lunch
Fourth period, AP Art History, Butler, Rm 108
Fifth period, AP English Literature and Composition, Steinberg, Rm G20
Sixth period, Advanced Figure Drawing, Vasquez, Rm G82
Seventh period, Women's Studies, McGinnis, Rm 157

Mina groaned. "I am a daisy trapped in the killing field of war."

"MINA LEE!"

It was clear that Saachi had reached the end of her patience. Mina hastened toward the large staircase.

"I am a cog in the education machine of mediocrity," Mina grumbled as she stomped up the stairs.

"Keep walking, cog," Saachi replied sharply.

• • •

The third-period bell rang, and Mina sped down the stairs and through the hallways for the first time since she'd stepped foot in school. She loved all her art classes, but this semester AP Studio Art was taught by her favorite teacher. Ms. Ellis was young and hip and not that much older than the seniors she taught.

A smile lit up Mina's face as she crossed from the monotonous void of high school drudgery into the vibrant chaos of the art room. She could smell the mix of old and new paint, both musty and milky wet, along with the pleasant chemical scent of turpentine. The sun had finally chased the rain clouds away and filled the room with bright natural light.

"Mina! So good to see you! How was your summer?"

Ms. Ellis had long straight brown hair that she kept in a loose ponytail and stylish black eyeglasses. What was most striking about her was the innate grace she seemed to exude, even when wearing a dirty paint-covered smock.

As they chatted, Mina let herself relax in the familiarity of her favorite classroom. She waved to a few old friends who were drawing in their sketchbooks and then went to sit down as Ms. Ellis greeted other arriving students.

Mina straddled the art horse at her usual spot next to the windows, which now shimmered with cascading streams of raindrops. She took a moment to stretch her back as she settled into her seat. Art horses were benches with movable drawing boards. While they were very practical, they were not at all comfortable.

All the students sat facing a large round table in the middle of the room. It was covered with an array of eclectic boxes that displayed a variety of interesting objects. Skulls, vases, antiques, tea sets, plates and jars filled with a mishmash of colorful stones, old toys, and small weird knickknacks. Satin fabrics and silk flowers were strewn in deliberate disarray. It was a display Mina could get lost in, providing hours of artistic inspiration. And that was the whole point.

Ms. Ellis made her assignments challenging and reminded Mina to think of art as more than just beautiful creations, but as things of power and structure and space. It was this belief in the importance of art that reminded Mina of her mother.

"Never forget, Mina. Art is magic," her mother told her.

And Mina had believed her. How could she not when she'd seen her mother breathe life into all her paintings?

Mina's mother had been a highly talented artist. She created realistic paintings that looked like vibrant photographs. It was her mother who taught her all about art from a young age. Put pencils and brushes in her hand. Let her roll her whole body in paint and decorate the walls of her art studio with handprints. Mina could communicate through drawing before she even learned to talk. It was in her blood.

"Hey, Mina! You're here!"

Mina saw Christina Jackson sit down in front of her, looking immaculate as usual, her black hair smoothed into a tight ponytail.

"I didn't think your dad would let you take this class," Christina continued.

Mina's face darkened, her lips tightening. "Yeah, he's not happy about it."

Christina frowned in sympathy. "I'm sorry, Mina. What are you going to do about art school applications?"

This was something that had been worrying Mina all summer. "I don't know. Maybe apply to universities with good art programs instead of just art schools?"

"But what about RISD? We talked about applying together."

Mina sighed. "He's fixated on me going to a 'real' college."

"Why don't you apply to the Brown/RISD program like I am? He can't possibly be against that."

Rolling her eyes, Mina snorted. "You've clearly mistaken me for someone else. I'm the Asian that's bad at math, remember? Brown would be offended if I applied to them. Unlike you, Miss Genius Jackson, sure to be valedictorian, who also happens to be a brilliant sculptor. All the top schools are gonna be fighting over you in one big nasty catfight. Rawr."

A flush spread on Christina's cheeks, giving her dark brown skin a rosy glow and highlighting the few freckles she had. Mina thought how cute her friend looked when she got embarrassed.

"That's not true," Christina demurred.

Mina pretended to talk into a mic. "Ms. Jackson, you've

been accepted to all the Ivies and fifty top schools across the world—where do you think you'll go?"

"Cut it out, Mina!" Christina laughed.

"No, the answer is whoever gives you the most money, of course!"

"Well, I'm hoping we both get accepted to RISD," Christina remarked.

"You'll definitely get in, but I don't know if RISD will even take me." The thought was depressing. It had been her first choice for a long time.

"Stop being so hard on yourself, Mina," Christina said. "You're smart and wicked talented. You can go to whatever school you want."

"Not if my dad won't let me." Mina grimaced.

"You've got to convince him! We've been taking art together for three years. I'd love to continue that in college."

"Yeah, me too," Mina replied. She loved having art with Christina not only because her friend was so talented, but because they challenged each other to do better.

"Oh, and I read your webcomic," Christina said, with a smile. "Your art's amazing."

"Really?" Mina beamed. "You must be, like, my third actual reader. It hasn't done well on Toonwebz." She'd been uploading a webcomic all summer on the popular online comics platform, thinking that if it became successful it would help convince her father that art school was worth it. But so far, it hadn't garnered many views.

"Your line art is really clean. Every panel is like a portrait. It must take you ages to do an episode—your art is so detailed!"

It was Mina's turn to flush. "Aw, thanks, Christina. That means a lot coming from you."

They turned their attention to Ms. Ellis as she began her welcome speech, but Mina was still thinking about her dad. He hadn't always been against art. He'd been her mother's greatest supporter. Bragged about how talented his wife was. Said he was also proud of Mina's art. But everything changed when her mother died three years ago.

It had happened so quickly. Her mom had gone out to get groceries on a rainy Saturday morning, and that was the last time Mina saw her. Someone ran a red light and slammed into her mother's car.

In his grief, her father packed away all her mother's creations. Art was too painful for him. At first, Mina understood. The mere whiff of linseed oil and paint thinner would stab her heart with such intense longing for her mother that it almost paralyzed her. But as time passed, she missed the bold vibrant colors of her mother's paintings, and she slowly brought them into her room. Art was Mina's way of staying connected to her mother.

"Mina, are you okay?"

Mina was startled to find Ms. Ellis standing next to her, a concerned look on her pretty face. The room was quiet, as all the students were busy sketching. But Mina's paper was blank.

"Yes, I'm fine." Mina smiled weakly.

"Are you having a problem with the assignment?"

Staring at her paper, Mina realized she hadn't heard what she was supposed to do.

"Um, uh . . ."

"Expressive self-portrait?"

Mina nodded. "Was just thinking about how to approach it," she answered.

Ms. Ellis nodded before moving on to Christina's work.

Mina looked around and could see that some students had snatched up the few handheld mirrors in the room while the rest were using their phone cameras. Ah, the beauty of art class, the only place where cell phones were actively encouraged. Mina pulled hers out, took a couple of selfies, and set the phone on her easel.

The key to portraits was how well the artist could depict emotions. It was Mina's mother who taught her to study people's faces to understand what every wrinkle conveyed.

"Every face tells a story," her mother would say. "Find the story that you want to share with the world."

Art made Mina look at people in a different way. Instead of the whole, she would focus on interesting aspects of a person's physique. The curve of their eyebrow, the delicate bones of their wrist, the subtle way they shifted their body, or their elusive dimple. Mina felt like she was in a constant state of observing others, all in her quest to perfect her art and tell a story. It was why she enjoyed creating her webcomic. Today, she had to turn that ability onto herself. Something she usually avoided at all costs.

Looking at her photos, she critically assessed them and began to sketch. Heart-shaped face, high cheekbones, average-sized nothing-special nose, half-moon eyes with a double eyelid on the right and a monolid on the left, and little bulges under her eyes that her mother used to call "aegyo sal," which is Korean for cute eye fat. Although "cute eye fat" seemed a weird compliment. It was her uneven eyes that Mina found the most interesting about her face. Her right eye was distinctly bigger, making her eyelashes jut out and appear longer than the lashes of her left eye. She could be a model for one of those double eyelid plastic surgery centers in South Korea. The left eye was the before and the right one the after. In fact, her paternal grandmother had wanted her to get double eyelid surgery on her left eye so she could be "pretty." Mina refused. She liked her uneven eyes. They made her unique. And she thought her monolid was just as pretty as her double eyelid. But what kind of story could she tell about them?

"Sometimes a face has yet to develop its story; sometimes you have to capture the promise of one."

Her mother's comments were often cryptic, but still, somehow, Mina understood what she meant. Not that she could explain it to anyone. It was just a feeling of knowing. Mina studied her selfies and thought, *My story has not yet begun, but it has great potential.*

The end-of-class bell rang and Mina had managed only a rough sketch. But she liked how she'd emphasized her eyes. They looked as if they had a lot to say.

CHAPTER 2

Best Friends

Lunch period was always a mass exodus of students charging out of school to hit up various fast food restaurants and the local grocery store. Mina always found it a colossal waste of energy. By the time you got your food, the period was almost over and you'd have to wolf it down before racing to your next class. Packing lunch was faster and healthier.

Mina followed Saachi into the courtyard. The sun was bright and no one could guess it had been dumping rain just hours ago. A trio of ninth-grade boys were already sitting at the bench by Mina and Saachi's favorite tree, a big beautiful red maple. Saachi walked over and gave them a withering stare. Mina watched as the ninth graders shriveled into human Sour Patch Kids before skulking away. They were both afraid of and in awe of Saachi. Who could blame them? Saachi was tall and beautiful with wavy black hair down to her waist.

Plopping onto the bench, Saachi smiled at the retreating boys.

"Is it wrong that I enjoy doing that?"

"Is it wrong that I enjoy watching you do that?"

The friends elbow-bumped each other in perfect harmony.

"This semester is going to suck so bad." Saachi sighed. "Ms. Fong just assigned a shit ton of homework today and I regret everything."

"And whose fault is that?" Mina was completely unsympathetic. "Who takes five AP courses senior year? A masochist, that's who."

"You're one to talk," Saachi retorted. "You're taking at least three APs."

"Please, you're in the hardest physics and calculus courses as well as Environmental Science, Stat, and Lit," Mina replied. "You are going to die."

"It's first semester senior year—we're supposed to be absolutely miserable."

"Yes, but when you have a cavity that just needs a filling, you don't ask the dentist for a root canal without anesthesia instead. Sick, I tell you."

"Don't judge me, I live my life on the edge." Saachi opened her lunch bag and began to sort several small containers of fruits and vegetables on the bench next to her.

Mina shook her head and tsked. "How can you be so tall existing on nothing but rabbit food?"

"Because cheese, my lactose intolerant friend," Saachi said.

"Jealous," Mina grumbled. "You don't know what I'd

give to eat as much pizza or ice cream as I want without running to the bathroom."

"Don't want to know." Saachi methodically shoveled grapes, cheese, olives, and crackers into her mouth in that order.

"Well, I guess you don't want any of my gim either." Mina waved a small rectangular package of roasted seaweed in Saachi's face.

With a high keening sound, Saachi grabbed the package and fondled it against her cheek. "My mom hasn't gone to Costco in a few weeks and I've been out of my precious!"

Guffawing, Mina tossed several more packages into Saachi's lap. "You don't need Costco—you have me, your friendly neighborhood seaweed dealer."

Saachi accepted the little rectangular packages with a smile.

"Thank you, best friend!"

Mina paused with a serious look. "But I don't know how to feel about Costco selling gim. It feels both weird and good. Something from my culture has gone mainstream American! And now white children everywhere are eating roasted seaweed, but without rice. Like potato chips. That's kind of wrong."

She opened a small bento box filled with Korean purple rice with beans, tiny anchovies, soy sauce, meat, and peppers.

"I still think it's wild that you can buy kimchi at Costco. And some of these bougie gourmet markets are making their own not-so-good versions," Saachi said. "They're right next to the frozen vegetable biryani."

"Ah, the stinky smell of cultural appropriation."

Mina shared her purple rice with her friend and accepted a bunch of grapes in return.

"Did you watch the last episode of *My Love, My Life*?" Saachi asked. "It was epic!"

Mina blew a loud raspberry. "Stopped watching it."

Her friend gasped. "But why?"

"I'm just so tired of the jerky mean guys as the main love interests."

"Yeah, but they're so sexy," Saachi said.

"Aw, come on! That last drama we watched, the nice guy was even better-looking than the main guy," Mina said.

"But the jerk was way sexier."

Mina put down her drink. "You see, this is the problem with our society! You've been brainwashed into thinking bad boys are sexy. Sometimes they are, but most of the time they're just assholes."

"Ooooooh, who's the asshole? Share!" Megan Sandler appeared, dragging a chair behind her and setting it in front of the bench. Megan, Saachi, and Mina had been best friends since they'd met in middle school. Megan always joked that she was their token white friend.

She sat and proceeded to stare in shock at Mina. "Woman, what did you do to your hair?"

"What, you don't like it?" Mina had spent nearly her entire Saturday at the salon dyeing her brown-black hair a dark silvery gray ombre.

"You're literally a BuzzFeed meme now! You know the one about rebellious East Asian girls and colored streaks in their hair."